Sword Art: Online Alternative
Gun Gale
VII
4th Squad Jam

Keiichi Sigsawa

ILLUSTRATION BY
Kouhaku Kuroboshi

SUPERVISED BY
Reki Kawahara

CONTENTS

Sword Art Online Alternative

GUN GALE ONLINE

VII

4th Squad Jam: Continue

DESIGN: BEE-PEE

Sword Art Online Alternative
GUN GALE ONLINE
VIII
4th Squad Jam: Continue

Keiichi Sigsawa

ILLUSTRATION BY
Kouhaku Kuroboshi

SUPERVISED BY
Reki Kawahara

YEN ON

NEW YORK

SWORD ART ONLINE Alternative Gun Gale Online, Vol. 8
KEIICHI SIGSAWA

Translation by Stephen Paul
Yen On edition edited by Carly Smith & Yen Press Editorial
Cover art by Kouhaku Kuroboshi

SWORD ART ONLINE Alternative Gun Gale Online Vol. VIII
©Keiichi Sigsawa / Reki Kawahara 2018
Edited by Dengeki Bunko
First published in Japan in 2018 by KADOKAWA CORPORATION, Tokyo.
English translation rights arranged with KADOKAWA CORPORATION, Tokyo, through TUTTLE-MORI AGENCY, INC., Tokyo.

English translation © 2021 by Yen Press, LLC

Yen On
150 West 30th Street, 19th Floor
New York, NY 10001

Visit us at yenpress.com
facebook.com/yenpress
twitter.com/yenpress
yenpress.tumblr.com
instagram.com/yenpress

First Yen On Edition: February 2021

Yen On is an imprint of Yen Press, LLC.
The Yen On name and logo are trademarks of Yen Press, LLC.

Library of Congress Cataloging-in-Publication Data
Names: Sigsawa, Keiichi, 1972– author. | Kuroboshi, Kouhaku, illustrator. | Kawahara, Reki, supervisor. | Paul, Stephen (Translator), translator.
Title: 4th Squad Jam: Continue / Keiichi Sigsawa ; illustration by Kouhaku Kuroboshi ; supervised by Reki Kawahara ; translation by Stephen Paul ; cover art by Kouhaku Kuroboshi.
Description: First Yen On edition. | New York : Yen On, 2018– | Series: Sword art online alternative gun gale online ; Volume 8
Identifiers: LCCN 2018009303 | ISBN 9781975327521 (v. 1 : pbk.) | ISBN 9781975353841 (v. 2 : pbk.) | ISBN 9781975353858 (v. 3 : pbk.) | ISBN 9781975353865 (v. 4 : pbk.) | ISBN 9781975353872 (v. 5 : pbk.) | ISBN 9781975353889 (v. 6 : pbk.) | ISBN 9781975315320 (v. 7 : pbk.) | ISBN 9781975315979 (v. 8 : pbk.)
Subjects: | CYAC: Fantasy games—Fiction. | Virtual reality—Fiction. | Role playing—Fiction. | BISAC: FICTION / Science Fiction / Adventure.
Classification: LCC PZ7.1.S537 Sq 2018 | DDC [Fic]—dc23
LC record available at https://lccn.loc.gov/2018009303

ISBNs: 978-1-9753-1597-9 (paperback)
        978-1-9753-1598-6 (ebook)

10 9 8 7 6 5 4 3 2 1

LSC-C

Printed in the United States of America

THE 4th SQUAD JAM
FIELD MAP

AREA 1 : Airport

AREA 2 : Town / Mall

AREA 3 : Swampland / River

AREA 4 : Forest

AREA 5 : Ruins

AREA 6 : Lake

AREA 7 : Craters

AREA 8 : Highway

Sword Art Online Alternative
GUN GALE ONLINE

Playback
of
SQUAD JAM

SYNOPSIS OF PART I

Shortly before the fourth Squad Jam was announced, Karen got dragged along to one of her father's work parties, where she met a man.

Fire Nishiyamada, who used his short stature as fuel for his rise in the business world, became smitten with Karen when she didn't laugh at him. Through her father, he sent a request to initiate a romantic relationship with her and eventually get married.

Karen turned him down, thinking it was too soon, but through unknown means, he learned that she was playing *GGO* as the character named Llenn. He even went to the trouble of registering his own avatar, Fire, to meet her in-game—what a bother.

When Fire revealed his distaste for VR games and his intention to make her quit *GGO* once they started dating, Llenn was furious. She intended to reject him at once. But Pitohui, who was present at their meeting, cleverly goaded her into making an agreement: If they fought in SJ4 and she died before he did, she would admit defeat and go out with him.

Upon realizing the consequences of her action, Llenn was stunned. But Pitohui simply said, "You can play dumb and pretend it never happened."

And then, SJ4 arrived.

Llenn was burning with excitement to finally have a real battle against her long-standing rivals, Team SHINC.

As usual, she grouped up with Pitohui, M, and Fukaziroh, with the one-time addition of Shirley and Clarence.

However, her elation at this dream team of balanced offense and defense was short-lived; Shirley and Clarence had only joined so they could skip the preliminary round. Llenn was crestfallen.

And in SJ4, there was a set of special rules: Monsters will appear if you remain in the same place for over five minutes. Shooting them will bring more of them. All ammo is fully replenished every thirty minutes as a way to balance out this challenge.

These rules were devised by the novelist sponsor—that creep. Everyone was pissed.

Team LPFM was given a disadvantageous starting position that set them up for a difficult fight.

They survived somehow, but then Shirley and Clarence split off, leaving them a team of four again.

Fifty minutes into the game, Llenn caught what was happening on the Satellite Scan.

A number of teams had joined together in an alliance. And among them was SHINC…

CHAPTER 7

What They Were Doing

SECT.7

CHAPTER 7
What They Were Doing

August 26th, 2026. Noon.

The fourth Squad Jam had just begun.

At that moment, Llenn opened her eyes in the southeast corner of the map and thought, *Starting in the forest again, huh?*

Meanwhile, in the northeast corner of the same map stood SHINC, whose members were all from the gymnastics team of the high school attached to Llenn's college.

A woman with the strength and stature of a gorilla, possessing the kind of burly face and body that would make a little child cry, looked upon a vast, wide-open runway and grunted.

"Grrr…"

She turned to look around, braids swaying, but all she saw was cracked asphalt that seemed to reach the horizon. The sky was clear overhead, glowing dull red.

Boss faced her teammates. "Everyone get down and watch the horizon. Snipers, shoot enemies on sight."

The visibility in the middle of the runway was excellent, but they had nothing nearby to use as cover. Dropping flat on the ground was their only option.

Her teammates complied immediately. Five women dressed in poisonous-looking green camo formed a circle, distanced themselves slightly, then hit the deck.

Tohma, the black-haired sniper, stood her Dragunov automatic sniper rifle on its bipod and took a peek through its adjustable scope. "What are we lookin' at today…?"

She was scanning the southwest. Across the runway and its sight lines, very far in the distance, there was a control tower that loomed like a high-rise building, and a terminal building like a low, squat fortress. They looked hazy in the distance.

In front of the terminal was an assortment of passenger jets in different sizes, resting on their wheels, or sometimes directly on their underbellies if the wheels had broken off—airplanes that would never fly again. Their tails stuck up like gravestones.

Next to Tohma was a short and squat woman, Sophie, who muttered, "Gosh, this airport sure is big. How often does someone get to walk down the middle of a runway?"

She wasn't holding a gun. That was because she was the carrier; the team's strongest armament, a PTRD-41 antitank rifle, and its ammo were snug in her inventory. It was an incredibly heavy weapon, so she couldn't also have her own machine gun at the ready.

Because the event organizer instructed them to bring a pistol for SJ4, she had an automatic Strizh pistol in a holster on her right hip, as did the other members.

Boss had ordered them to fire at will because the PTRD-41 was capable of sending one of its rounds over a kilometer away: the minimum possible distance between any two teams at the start.

They'd gone to great pains to acquire that weapon so they could destroy M's shield in SJ2, and it had played a major role in both SJ2 and SJ3. Its 14.5 mm rounds were almost certainly the largest you could find in *GGO* at the moment.

It wasn't a pure sniper rifle, so after a few hundred yards, its accuracy took a major dive, but the important part was that it still hit with lethal force, which was certainly true.

If any nearby teams weren't paying attention, Sophie could attack them without fear of reprisal. She could also use the gun's bullet line to push them around. While they panicked and went on the defensive, the other members could approach and finish off the targets separately.

However, despite having the capability to actually use this strategy, Tohma finished checking the vicinity through her scope and declared, "No other teams in visible range. Darn!"

The rule was that every other team would be at least three-fifths of a mile away at the start of the game, but that didn't mean they would be *exactly* that distance. Since the visibility was so good here, they must've been placed much farther away.

"Can't see anything here, either," reported Rosa. She was the middle-aged redhead on the opposite position from Tohma. The woman was quite tall and solidly built, though not as much as Boss. She was holding the Russian masterpiece, a PKM machine gun.

"Are we at the very edge of the map again, ya think?" asked a boyish woman at Rosa's side. This woman was Tanya, and she had short silver hair and narrow, foxy eyes.

She was a bit of a tomboy in real life and accentuated that characteristic in *GGO*. Every now and then, her real-life self poked out in speech, but that was just part of the charm. Plenty of times, her teammates didn't even notice.

Tanya dumped most of her points into agility, so she was the fastest on the team—though not to as extreme an extent as Llenn.

She liked to use a PP-19 Bizon submachine gun for its compact size and fast fire rate. It contained distinctive cylindrical magazines that held fifty-three 9 mm Parabellum rounds for pistols. Hers was equipped with a silencer, which reduced the noise from her shots.

So Tanya made up for her lack of range and power with speed, fire rate, and a silencer that helped conceal her location.

"I suppose so. We should probably take that as a compliment to our strength," agreed blond and beautiful Anna, who always wore sunglasses. She was keeping an eye out with her binoculars.

Like Tohma, she used a Dragunov sniper rifle, but this one only had the normal 4× zooming scope, which was how you could tell the guns apart.

Tohma handled the longer sniping, while Anna was good at the kind of sniping that involved rapid repositioning and shooting. That was something her player, Moe Annaka, could do because of her agility. She seemed soft and cuddly, but she had the quickest reflexes of anyone on the gymnastics team.

"Hmm..."

Boss was low and flat on the runway, large backpack holding her silenced rifle, the Vintorez. She didn't put the Vintorez in a sling, preferring to keep her arms unobstructed when running. Instead, she normally kept it in her backpack when it wasn't in her hands. And that was usually when she had her binoculars out to give orders as the team leader.

Sprawled out on the ground like a sunning sea lion, Boss peered at her Satellite Scan terminal. The little screen displayed a map of the battle arena, and a single illuminated point marked their present location in the northeast corner.

"Everyone, listen up," she said. "We're in the northeast corner of the map. No enemies to the north or east."

That caused the other members to readjust their positions accordingly. They were all looking for foes to the south and west now.

"We'll take shifts for the lookout. When you're off, check the map and memorize the surrounding features," Boss said, switching back to her binoculars. Everyone took turns watching the Satellite Scan, paying close attention to their battleground.

The ability to quickly memorize a map that you might not have the luxury of looking at again soon was one of the qualifications to being a good Squad Jam player.

At 12:02, Sophie sidled up next to Boss once she'd learned the features of the map and asked, "We gonna wait here until the scan?"

"I think so... Unless they have an antimateriel rifle, this isn't a bad spot. In fact, we might be better off just staying here."

"What if that little pink rabbit comes charging at us through the smoke?" Sophie asked with a piercing smile. Boss flashed her pearly whites back.

"Let's hope she does," she said. "We'll wait here until the ten-minute mark. Don't get bored and fall asleep, now."

Everyone smiled or chuckled at that—but three minutes later, they were doing anything but smiling.

✳   ✳   ✳

Noon.

Memento Mori, frequently abbreviated to MMTM, started at the northwest corner of the map.

They were in the midst of a ruined city, a metropolis that looked like it had been picked up and shaken three times. Most of the buildings were decrepit but still stood bravely, while those that had learned how to rest had collapsed sideways.

The wide roads were littered with rubble and vehicles that would never again pass a safety inspection, but the paths were clear and visible for the most part.

Amid the urban grid was a straight set of tracks, not elevated on supports but simply laid on raised ground. It was just two parallel tracks, meaning it was a single line. Atop the tracks was a very large locomotive, sitting inactive.

It had a diesel engine, the kind built in the United States and exported to countries around the world. There was a fictional railroad's logo on it, and the exterior paint was chipped and rusty.

But even a diesel train didn't run entirely on its engine. First the motor had to be engaged with electric power. The locomotive was over seventy feet long and weighed 180 tons—a true monster.

"In the corner again. Well, I knew that would happen," said David, MMTM's team leader, as he glared at the Satellite Scanner and the scenery around them. "Kenta and Summon, climb up to the roof of the blue building on the left. Survey the area and remember the terrain. Report if you see an enemy, but do not open fire—come down at once. Jake and Lux, get up on the tracks and keep an eye on the south. If you see someone, *do* open fire. Bold, stick with me. Take turns checking the map."

The rest of the team chimed in to indicate that they understood their orders.

Of course, they were a smart enough team to react accordingly regardless, but it was the leader's job to put these things into firm words. That way, any confusion or mistaken assumptions could be eliminated for good.

Their (virtual) lives were on the line. Team MMTM worked on a professional, clinical framework: no negligence, no guesswork.

Jake the machine gunner and Lux the sniper moved in front of the train and lay down on the tracks, where they had the best visibility and firing position. They set up their HK21 machine gun and MSG90 automatic sniper rifle on bipods side by side, respectively. These two weapons were based on the same G3 assault rifle body and shot the same 7.62 mm bullets—deadly ones that were powerful while still being accurate at nearly nine hundred yards.

David and Bold scanned the horizon with their assault rifles. David used the Austrian Steyr STM-556, with a grenade launcher attached beneath its barrel, while Bold preferred the Italian Beretta ARX160.

Kenta and Summon, who used a German G36K and a Belgian FN Herstal SCAR-L, respectively, vanished through the doorway of a tall building nearby.

All four of their armaments used the same standardized 5.56 × 45 mm NATO rounds. Even their magazines were the same, so the packs they held in the pouches on their backs weren't for themselves, but for their teammates to pull out and use when reloading.

As previously, they wore a Swedish military camo uniform, colored in various shades of green in angular patterns. On their shoulders were patches bearing their team logo: a skull with a knife in its jaws.

Their other accessories, like belts, suspenders, and magazine pouches, were almost identical to previous events, but with one notable difference: In accordance with the special rules of SJ4, they all had a pistol equipped, too.

The team was well-versed in long-range guns, so they hardly ever used pistols, which were weak, close-range weapons. They preferred an aggressive approach, fighting with their rifles indoors and outdoors.

That was purely by choice, however. David was the only exception, with an M9-A1 9 mm pistol made by Steyr, the same as his rifle.

But the special rules made it clear that these items were now mandatory. So each member carried an automatic Beretta APX on his right side, where his dominant hand could reach it. The guns fired 9 mm Parabellum rounds, with seventeen shots to a magazine.

Of course, they knew that merely *having* the pistols wasn't the point. They'd taken the time to practice shooting several hundred rounds to ensure they were comfortable using the guns.

Just after 12:02, Kenta and Summon had finished climbing the stairs and gotten into lookout positions, where they soon reported that no enemies were in a visible range. All members declared that they'd had time to check the map and memorize its features.

"Good. After the first scan, we're leaving these city ruins. I don't dislike the terrain, but it'll work against us if we have to deal with someone like the pink shrimp," David instructed his team. "We'll defeat any enemy teams as we move—clockwise from the north. We'll move as soon as the scan is done. There's bound to be a dangerous team in the northeast, so be careful."

When the others chimed in that they understood, MMTM officially began the most famous of Squad Jam tactics: hunkering down on high alert until the first scan arrived.

From Bold, the team member who wore his hair in locs, came the message, "Leader! This thing can run!" He'd used his downtime to examine the vehicle, apparently.

"Ahhh… I'll go take a look. Keep watching out, everyone," said David, and he began trotting toward the engine.

It was pointed to the south. He climbed up the ladder on the rear of the locomotive, then used the inside passageway to proceed up to the engineer's seat. Right there on the illuminated control panel was a fuel gauge indicating there was plenty left.

But David promptly announced, "We're not using this."

The tracks pointed slightly to the southeast, in fact, in a five o'clock direction that continued all the way to the bottom edge of the map. Using the train would allow them to cross that six-mile distance very quickly, but it would make them the perfect target to any nearby teams that could shoot at them.

The big, hardy locomotive itself could withstand some gunshots, but a blast from a plasma grenade could easily destroy the rails. If they went out, the train would easily derail. Because it was so heavy, it wouldn't be able to stop in time. And the faster it traveled, the worse the accident would be.

If this were the end of Squad Jam and there were few enemies remaining, he might have chosen to use it. That was because quickly traveling long distances in between scans was very advantageous for catching an enemy by surprise.

But now that he had decided not to use the locomotive, that left only one thing to do.

"Leave plenty of souvenirs, Bold. We get automatic refills this time, so don't hold back."

"Got it!"

Bold removed seven ordinary detonation grenades from his inventory and placed them atop the ladder on the back of the train, the entrance to the cab, underneath the driver's seat, and near the wheels.

If anyone approached without due caution and hit the tiny wires, they'd pull the safety pins and detonate the grenades. The bit under the driver's seat was especially tricky: One was placed in a visible location and would set off a more carefully hidden grenade when removed.

"Kenta and Summon, head back. When the scan comes in, we'll move," said David. He checked the watch he wore on the inside of his left wrist. It was 12:04.

At 12:05, another one of the game's special rules went into effect.

Nearly every team was visited by one of the scout monsters. If they chose to shoot the creature dead, it would summon a much larger horde of them, which startled players all over the map.

SHINC was no exception.

"Dammit!" swore Tanya, who had gleefully dispatched the scout monster with her Bizon. "So this is the special rule, huh?! This is why they're refilling our ammo!" Now the Amazons were surrounded by an invasion of monsters out in the middle of a wide-open space with no shelter.

"That sick, twisted writer! He came up with this to mess with us!" snarled Boss, aiming with her Vintorez. "We can't get ourselves killed right here at the start! That would be pathetic! No, let's do some warm-ups and blow 'em all away! Sophie, I want you to pay attention to the perimeter! Catch any enemies that might be trying to sneak up on us!"

The rest of the team called back. They were already in a state of open fire, so they probably wouldn't have heard her if not for their in-ear communication pieces.

"Rah-rah-rah-raaah!" cried Rosa, her PKM blasting deep and sharp. In between shots, the two Dragunovs howled, while the two guns with silencers were completely inaudible.

This was how SHINC ended up killing monsters in a frenzy until after the scan had passed.

"I see. So that's how this works..."

In contrast to SHINC, MMTM was very careful.

David didn't want to shoot the scout monster and make noise, so he chose to slice it open with his lightsword.

No other enemies appeared after that. The coast was quiet.

While he wondered why a monster had shown up, David heard gunshots in the distance and quickly put the picture together for himself.

"It's a nasty trap. If you shoot the first scout without thinking, a whole bunch of them attack. Just the sort of thing that piece of crap writer would come up with," he grunted, figuring out the trap as quickly as Pitohui had.

"Nice one, Leader. Or 'Nicelee' for short. So what now?" asked Jake, who was on his stomach, cradling the HK21. He suggested, "The team to the southeast is close. Should we whack 'em?"

They could hear the fighting over the tracks, which offered a long open space to collect sound, such as a distant team shooting more monsters. That was probably the closest team to them at the start of the game. If they rushed over, they could easily defeat that team while they were occupied by the creatures.

David shook his head, though. "No. We'll wait it out."

"Okay. How come?" Jake wondered. Normally, David would choose the merciless option.

"Change of plans," the leader said at once. "This Squad Jam, we're not taking any chances at the start. Let the others wear themselves out killing monsters. We'll attack for five minutes, starting at twenty-five after. It'll be harder for them to fight back just before the ammo refill."

Jake flashed his pearly whites.

"Nicelee. That's ruthless."

At 12:06, all over the battlefield, huge swarms of monsters were startling and vexing players who did not expect to see them—but there was one group cheering as loudly as their gunfire.

"So many enemies! So many targets!"

"This is so much fuuuuun!"

"What a crazy special rule! I love this game!"

"This is awesome! Keep firing!"

"Hya-haaa! Rock 'n' roll, man!"

Indeed, it was none other than the All-Japan Machine-Gun Lovers, whose team abbreviation was ZEMAL.

Their starting point was the southwest corner of the map. Yes, they were considered one of the top four squads for SJ4 and thus relegated to one of the corners.

But they didn't give that much thought. They were too busy shooting away.

In the midst of an unreal landscape—a wasteland full of craters caused by bombardment or perhaps a swarm of meteors—five machine guns outfitted with a belt-loading system, which allowed hundreds of rounds to be fired in succession, were at full roar.

"Ryaaaaaa!"

Zudu-du-du-du-du-du-du-du-du-doom!

The merciless gunfire exhibited exactly what the automatic weapon was designed to do. A hailstorm of bullets tore through the flock of monsters besieging the team.

"Max, cover Shinohara as he replaces his barrel."

"Yes, my goddess!"

Among the burly, manly men was a pure, feminine voice.

"Huey, there's a group of them on the left. Those are all yours."

"Got it! Ura-ra-raaaa!"

"Tomtom, once you've defeated yours, go up to the lip of the crater behind us and keep an eye on the perimeter as you change your barrel. Peter, cover him."

"Gotcha, ma'am!"

The woman they'd carried into the bar on their shoulders was now standing in the middle of the group, giving orders. And they were sharp and snappy orders, indeed.

She had the three gunners with 7.62 mm weapons, the bulk of the team's firepower, moving around to different positions and switching their overheated barrels when appropriate, and the two 5.56 mm gunners filled the gaps.

It was a very effective, powerful, and beautiful strategy that made the most of ZEMAL's ability—though the actual men who were faithfully carrying out their goddess's directives likely weren't capable of understanding or appreciating this.

"Damn, these guys are incredible…"

As usual, the crowd watching the action from the bar had a bird's-eye view of the situation, a vista far superior to what those actually fighting could see. And what they saw was a ZEMAL at its peak. They were the stars of the screen.

The crowd was here to see action, and they spared no praise for the players who put on a show.

"When did those machine-gun idiots outfit themselves with those nifty backpack-loading ammo systems…?"

"It's not fair, right? They can blast at pretty much anyone for as long as they want!"

"And they've got even more than that this time…"

"Yeah."

The eyes of the crowd were naturally drawn to the pretty woman wearing a beanie at their center.

She hadn't fired a single shot from the RPD machine gun hanging from her shoulder because she'd been issuing orders the entire time. She was bold, precise, and intelligent.

"She's a brilliant tactician. I guess that when it comes to idiots and machine gunners, it's all in how you use them…"

"They're the same thing in this case."

"Good point. Sorry."

It was 12:09. After all the action and chaos, the final monster on the screen was shot and vanished.

Many teams had appeared on the monitors doing battle with the monster hordes, but ZEMAL finished them off quickest of all.

It was about to be 12:10 in Japan, in *GGO*, and in the battlefield of SJ4.

Only two teams succeeded in destroying all of their invading monsters by the first Satellite Scan.

The first of them was, of course, ZEMAL.

As for the other...

"Opticals are the best!"

"Dang, man, this is too sweet!"

"Fire, fire, fire!"

"Wah-ha-ha-ha-ha!"

The Ray Gun Boys, abbreviated RGB, exclusively used optical guns, and like ZEMAL, they were blasting away without a care in the world.

The futuristic optical weapons unique to *GGO* had a plethora of benefits: They were lightweight and fired both rapidly and accurately, unaffected by the wind, for a long duration thanks to their energy packs. But they also had one critical downside: Defensive fields in PvP reduced their power significantly.

In other words, they were the most effective weapons to use on a sudden stream of fairly weak monsters.

They weren't fazed in the least by a wall-to-wall surge of monsters around them. They sprayed bullets of light at the onrushing creatures like water from a hose, reducing them to showers of polygonal shards.

Standing atop the frozen lake, they put on as good a show as ZEMAL did.

Meanwhile, from a prone position atop a highway bordering the lake, a man peered through binoculars, watching the fireworks exhibition.

He wore a venomous-looking original design of camo, a thin mask of green material, and a single-lens pair of sunglasses. His face was completely hidden.

The man muttered, "Those guys could be useful... I'll invite them to the group."

By 12:13, nearly all the teams had finished their initial battle with the monsters.

The number of total monsters spawned seemed to be the same, regardless of location, and the fights all lasted six to eight minutes.

A few unfortunate groups were unable to defend against the waves of claws and fangs, so they found themselves out of the game. It had to be very humiliating to enter a competitive event against other players and end up torn to shreds by disgusting, unthinking monsters instead.

Faster-moving competitors wiped out some other, equally unfortunate teams while they were distracted with the monsters— just like ZAT, who had been on the wrong end of a battle with Llenn's squad.

As for SHINC, who had to fight on the wide-open runway, Boss and the others were perfectly unharmed. Not a single one of them suffered any damage from the monsters.

"That was a hardcore warm-up…"

But it did require quite a number of bullets to get through. Without any cover, they didn't have the luxury of drawing their foes closer for a more accurate shot. They just had to keep firing until the creeps were gone.

Boss called for each member to report her ammo status. Most of them were down to about half their original stock—60 percent at the highest. It was what they had to do to survive, but this was a tough situation to be pushed into right at the start of Squad Jam.

They all kept low to the ground, watching for any sign of enemy attack. Boss pulled a fresh magazine out of her inventory and grunted. "We get our ammo back at the half-hour mark… Gotta avoid battle until then."

Sophie scowled. "Exactly. We can't go up against Llenn in this state. What should we do, Boss?"

Boss slapped the new magazine into her Vintorez and pulled the loading handle. With the pleasant sound of metal sliding on metal, the next bullet fit into the chamber. With its silencer on, the Vintorez fired so quietly that the reload alone seemed loud.

"I'm guessing the monsters show up if you stay in one spot for more than five minutes. It's designed to keep you from camping. As long as we stay on the move, it shouldn't be a problem. The *actual* problem is that we're too exposed here. I want to get out of this area. We're changing plans. Tanya, Tohma."

The two women turned to her, and she continued, "Look for a vehicle. There's probably something near the airport terminal. Tanya takes the lead, and Tohma follows about three hundred yards behind. If you don't find anything by twelve twenty, come back. Everyone else, wait for now. After four minutes, we'll move slowly to the north."

"Roger that! Let's go!"

"Hey, don't get too far ahead!"

Tanya was the fastest member of the team, and Tohma was the only one who actually knew how to drive a manual transmission in real life. They rushed off down the runway.

Before long, Tanya was just a dot in the distance. Tohma and her long Dragunov followed behind at a more realistic pace.

If the two of them ran into a full enemy group of six, they wouldn't stand a chance.

But that was by design.

If *someone* had to run reconnaissance, they might as well limit the potential damage in a losing fight. If Tanya got shot from her forward position, Tohma would be far enough behind that she could turn around and run back to the group.

As the point person of the team, Tanya accepted the risk of being the first one shot in any battle, and she had the duty of reporting enemy location, numbers, and gun types before she died. Whether she went down without saying anything or died after informing the team made a huge difference in how they could react.

Being a good point person in *GGO* meant knowing the types of guns in the game by appearance—even better if you recognized them by sound. It's not like you could tell the bullet type or distance solely from the pain of being shot, after all.

And giving orders that might very well end in the death of one or two teammates was the job of the team leader.

Such a leader put a hand to her left ear. She temporarily switched off her comm so she wouldn't accidentally talk over the two scouts, and she whispered, "Now we just pray that they find something."

"Yes. It's a hardcore setup this time," Sophie agreed, approaching quietly and turning off her comm, too, so they could speak directly in person.

Boss glanced at her reliable partner and grinned.

"But it's just as tough for Llenn's team."

While Boss was in the distant northeast corner of the battleground, smirking in a way guaranteed to terrify any small child, there was another team a few miles to the west, in the midst of a ruined city, silently making their way forward and communicating only through physical gestures.

"……"

"……"

Of course, the only team that could achieve this level of coordination was MMTM.

They were among massive buildings that had toppled over sideways without breaking apart. This was impossible in real life; if a building this tall lost its balance, it would simply crumble to the ground.

MMTM swiveled and peered not just ahead and to the sides, but toward the windows and rooftops of other buildings, wary of attacks, ensuring they had no blind spots as they hurried down the street.

They were as smooth and efficient as could be, like leaves flowing atop a river as they wove between the rocks breaking the surface.

They spoke not a single word so they could more easily hear

any noises that another team might carelessly make. And of course, it was also to ensure they could hear gunfire and bullets coming their way.

With all the attacks that *GGO* players suffered from monsters and other players, those with skill gradually learned what distance and direction the bullets were coming from by senses alone.

The comm item that allowed constant dialogue was very convenient, but newer players tended to rely on it too much and disregard their own ears. And if the team was engaged in too much idle chatter, they could very easily miss the sound of the enemy.

Any good team had to know that in places where hostile encounters were expected, the leader would only give the necessary minimum of orders, and the other members would engage in the necessary minimum of communication.

"…"

Kenta, on point, held his G36K at shoulder height, keeping the muzzle perfectly level as he moved. A fallen building formed a wall on the right, hiding him from anyone beyond it.

When he reached the exposed foundation of the building at the corner, he deftly switched the gun to his left hand and peered around the side. Once he was certain there were no enemies present, he waved up Bold and gave a sign that it was safe to proceed.

MMTM flowed through the ruins.

Since they didn't need to deal with the monsters, they had much more time than the others. With the barbed wire on the metal pole fencing—the northern edge of the map—on their left side, they moved quickly to the east.

They continued onward like ninjas until shortly before the 12:20 scan, and they did not come into contact with a single enemy team.

It was 12:20.

"Here we go! Time for the second scan!"

On the big screen in the bar, the squads' locations and names appeared one after the other. If they were still alive, they would be bright dots. Gray blips were for those who'd been taken out. There were numbers to the side, too.

All told, the windowpane grid map showed that twenty-one teams were still alive. Nine were dead.

LPFM, SHINC, MMTM, and ZEMAL were still in it, which was a relief to the crowd.

"Shoulda figured that the toughest teams would pass that test with ease."

"I don't wanna see my sweet Llenn get killed by some worthless monsters."

"Seriously. Also, I know I say this every time, but she's not yours."

"You know what? You're right. She's *ours*."

"I won't deny that."

"You won't?!"

The displayed location of Llenn's team was at the south end of the map, prompting one of the usual arguments over her from the crowd, but that aside, the attention was mostly on the north side, where two groups were on a crash course.

"MMTM and SHINC look kinda close, don't they?"

MMTM started in the northwest corner, and SHINC in the northeast. Both were heading straight along the north edge of the map, meaning they were quickly closing the gap between them.

At 12:20, SHINC was on the left edge of the airport, and MMTM was on the right edge of the ruins. Only a mile of distance and the highway going through the center of the map separated the two.

"They might collide!"

"I do think they might!"

"Uh-oh, watch out!"

But the men in the bar were more expectant than worried.

*   *   *

"So it's MMTM…"

Boss was sitting in the passenger seat. But not in any ordinary vehicle.

It was a midsize truck about twenty-five feet long, with a large set of stairs in the bed: a special vehicle commonly known as an airstairs truck. These were the automobiles found only at airports, meant to be situated next to a plane on the runway so passengers could climb the stairs to get inside the cabin.

Slightly earlier, around 12:15, Tanya's cannonball charge into the airport terminal vicinity bore fruit, as she almost immediately found the airstairs truck.

Of course, it was Tohma who drove the truck once she caught up. It was an automatic transmission, though, so it wasn't that hard anyway.

SHINC regrouped and began to travel in their new set of wheels.

Two of them sat in the front seat. The other four were in the back—on top of the steps. The stairs had tall walls on either side, but no canopy on top. They rose high and tilted, to ensure they could reach the aircraft door.

Since different airplanes had different heights, the positioning of the stairwell could be adjusted up or down. Currently, they came to a height of about thirteen feet.

Having an elevation that high in a wide, flat area like this was a major advantage. Set up side by side on the top step were Rosa and her PKM machine gun along with Tohma and her PTRD-41 antitank rifle, while Sophie watched through binoculars from directly behind them. If she could spot any distant enemies, they could blast them from here.

Tanya was the one person left out of the fun, sitting at the base of the truck and singing to herself as she watched their six. "I'm the lonely, lonely leftover. All alone am I…"

The airstairs truck, which they'd transformed into a mobile gun turret complete with machine gun and antitank rifle, cruised easily to the west across the airport runway.

If they spotted any enemies, they were ready to pummel them with a hail of lead—but until 12:20, they did not spot anything moving across the wide-open asphalt.

"They must have escaped to the terminal. Or outside the airport entirely," said Boss.

They stopped the truck with ten seconds to go before the scan—at which point they learned that MMTM was close.

Boss asked her teammates up above, "MMTM's supposed to be at the edge of the ruins a mile to the west. Can anyone see them?"

From the very top of the stairs, Sophie said, "Nope. I can see the highway and the buildings, but not any people."

Tohma chimed in, "I don't see anything through my scope, either."

"Got it. Don't expose yourself to danger. But if you see them, you can fire," ordered Boss. Then she stopped to think, murmuring silently to herself.

She didn't expect to fight MMTM so early. Honestly, it wasn't something she wanted to get into now.

The ultimate goal of the battle royale was to win it all, of course, so MMTM was a foe they would clash with eventually and need to fight—but there was a foe they wanted to fight and beat more than them: Llenn.

However, according to the scan, the little pink bunny was on the south edge of the map. She was very far away. More time would have to pass before they could trade shots with her.

Before that, what to do about MMTM? As long as they were on the runway, the airstairs truck was a great advantage. They could aim from a height over flat land. What's more, there was still plenty of fuel.

But MMTM was too savvy not to figure that out quickly and respond with a counterstrategy. They might attempt to pop the tires first. Their leader's grenade launcher might shoot a smoke grenade to block their visibility so the enemy could pull closer. Maybe they'd aim for the fuel tank. Perhaps all of these at once.

If she could come up with these plans, she knew that MMTM would be capable of them— and perhaps be capable of something even smarter.

After several long seconds of consideration, Boss told the group her plan.

"We'll avoid combat with MMTM. This is the end of our leisurely drive for today," she said, then added, "Tanya, get out the duct tape. Rosa, change the PKM barrel. And I'll…"

At 12:20, learning that SHINC was their closest enemy via the scan, David grinned fiercely.

"We couldn't ask for a better opponent. Let's go and introduce ourselves—before we kill them."

He mentioned the introduction because, in the bar before the start of SJ2, Boss had told him, *I do hope you gentlemen will introduce yourselves before you get killed.*

David came off as the coolheaded type, but after his experiences against SHINC and Pitohui, he had a tendency to hold on to grudges.

"Roger that!" said the rest of the squad. They were pumped up to face off against SHINC.

According to the scan, a number of teams were gathered toward the center of the map. If they were in a melee rather than a team-up, joining the fight was an option, but they chose to ignore the clump for now.

"Leapfrog to the highway. Go," said David, referring to an alternative movement strategy.

While three members stayed at the ready to fire at any target, the other three advanced quickly past them before they switched positions. It was an alternating pattern of pausing and rushing, movement and standby. Obviously, if anyone came into contact with the enemy, combat would ensue.

MMTM used this tactic to break through the rest of the ruins and reach the highway. There were no hostile squads.

Before their eyes was a wide, massive highway structure.

The game's design was based on the United States of America, so it wasn't a raised highway. In Japan, such capacious paths would often be elevated so that intersecting surface roads could run beneath them, but it was typically the other way around over there.

The street was made of finely cracked gray concrete, four lanes for each direction. And each lane itself was quite wide, so when you added the shoulders and everything, it was a good hundred yards to cross the entire structure.

There were cars all over, some burned, some flipped over, some cut directly in half somehow. But for the most part, it felt pretty empty. There was plenty of visibility in every direction.

The center divider was a block wall of white concrete, about three feet tall and maybe a foot thick. Here and there, parts were missing, like a child's mouth full of teeth.

It was easy to see a depression running along the opposite side of the highway through the missing teeth. It was deep enough that a person could stand inside it without being seen. And after a slope of damp earth was a fence with holes here and there, beyond which you could see the airport.

"Okay, go!"

As the machine gunners and snipers watched the vicinity, speedy Kenta crossed first. He moved in a sprint, not bothering to look or ready his gun. If he got shot, so be it. He'd just have to pray that his teammates backed him up with maximum firepower.

And in the end, he was untouched. Nothing from the road; nothing from the airport.

Kenta hid in the depression, took a quick look around, and called, "All clear! No hostiles!"

"Bold, go!"

Bold was the next to proceed. The entire team sprinted across the highway, one at a time.

There was a variety of ways to cross dangerous open territory like roads and shallow rivers. They could have gone two at a time, or more—even the rest of them at once.

It made the crossing quicker, but at the risk of a single machine-gun sweep or well-placed grenade wiping out the entire team. It all came down to personal preference.

"Summon, go!"

MMTM chose to run over one at a time.

When they saw MMTM crossing the highway, the audience in the bar began to predict what would happen next, as was their wont.

Two men standing at a tall table with their drinks conversed. "A showdown between the skull team and SHINC. Exciting!"

"If the airport is the battlefield, the Amazons have the advantage. You saw them in that airstairs truck, right? They can shoot down from above."

"But the truck sticks out from a distance. If it's moving, they'll know SHINC's riding it. It's the perfect target for MMTM to hit. And you know a team that talented will find an easy way to win that battle."

"But that's it!"

"What's it?"

"The Amazons can simply stop the truck. If they hide behind a stationary vehicle, the other guys will think it's abandoned and come over, right? Then SHINC can blast 'em."

"That's pretty optimistic of you. What makes you think the skull team will goof up that badly?"

"Oh? You wanna bet on MMTM, then? I'll take the Amazons. How about we go big? I say a thousand credits."

"Sounds good to me. You're on!"

Since the laws of Japan didn't apply in this virtual place, the two began a friendly wager.

In a few minutes, both of them would be very disappointed.

At 12:25, David and the rest of MMTM waited on hands and knees atop the slope in front of a rusted, tattered fence. They stood before a vast open space of runways, taxiways, and the dirt tracts between them. The horizon was faded in the distance. More clouds hung in the sky now, and the wind was picking up.

From their position on the ground, they began observing the terrain.

The area ahead was so exposed that they couldn't move through it without a plan. Especially because SHINC had that antitank rifle. If they were carefully lying in wait somewhere, that would be very dangerous. In fact, it seemed like it might be impossible to spot them, if that were the case.

But then Lux, looking through the scope of his sniper rifle, reported, "East to southeast! There's a car on the move!" Apparently, it wasn't that hard after all. "It's an airstairs truck. Distance of twelve hundred yards. Approaching slowly from the right, up ahead. Crossing to the left side."

David followed this report by setting his scope's zoom to the maximum. Then he placed it along the slope and peered carefully through it.

"Got it."

It was hazy, being a very long distance away, but he could see them.

A truck with a large set of stairs on top of it was rolling along over the runway from the east-southeast, sticking out like a sore thumb. It wasn't going much more than five miles per hour.

Based on the locations of all teams in the last scan, it was almost certainly SHINC behind the wheel.

David kept watching. There was no visible figure in the driver's seat. They were probably leaning low and out of sight to avoid being shot through the windshield, and very slowly operating the pedals and wheel. It was probably quite awkward, but with a teammate spotting you, it wasn't impossible to do.

As for the top of the stairs, they were elevated, and the car was on a diagonal angle from here, so the wall blocked the view of the steps.

Even still, he could make out a narrow rod extending just a little bit. That was the barrel of one of SHINC's PKMs. And it meant they were using the top of the stairs as a machine-gun turret.

David grunted to himself while Lux described the vehicle to the rest of the team.

The last thing they wanted to do was get too close and have that weapon blasting at them from a secure spot up top. Battle would be very difficult on this flat runway with nowhere to hide. And SHINC had that antitank rifle, too.

Even worse, they had the mobility of a vehicle. If the tide of battle turned against them, they could easily put more space between the two teams with a little added pressure on the gas pedal.

The circumstances were against MMTM. But David didn't want to give up on combat and simply run away, either. This was a chance to fight against a worthy opponent without anyone else getting in the way. Plus, it wasn't a smart move to leave that set of airstairs in enemy hands.

Worst of all was the thought of finishing up Squad Jam and having those Amazons say, *Oh? You had a chance to fight us, and you ran away? That was a brilliant idea. You're savvy when it comes to self-preservation. We applaud you.*

So how did a team conquer a moving fortress on flat land without any cover while receiving a minimum of damage? David's mind raced to find the answer.

When bullets started flying in *GGO*, combat was like a game of fast chess. You had no time to think. The only thing you could do was act.

In three seconds, he asked, "Lux, can you hit that truck's fuel tank?"

"Nope. I looked for it, but I can't see it. Must be on the other side."

"Can you snipe the tires, then? I want to slow it down."

"Maybe if it gets down to six hundred yards. It's at eight hundred now!"

"Okay. Once it travels another hundred to the left, let it close within five hundred, then pop its tires at will. Bold, stick with Lux and watch for bullet lines from the staircase."

They replied affirmatively and began to run through the depression to the left-hand side where SHINC was going: north.

David continued, "If the car stops, I'll shoot a smoke grenade in front of it. But we're not all charging it—just making them *think* we are. Jake, you lay down covering fire near the car through the gas. I'll be the only one getting closer, and when the smoke clears, I'll shoot all the ordinary grenades I have. Kenta, Summon, if the car gets destroyed, I'll order you to rush it, depending on circumstantial factors. Be on the lookout until then."

His explanation concerned Kenta, who asked, "Why are you the only one undertaking all the danger?"

David grinned fiercely. "So I can hog all the glory."

12:28.

"Distance, five hundred. Here we go."

From his prone position immediately behind the fence, Lux began to snipe with the MSG90.

With a sharp report, it sent a 7.62 mm bullet flying over the wide-open airport runway at low altitude. It crossed the distance to the target in eight-tenths of a second, striking the front left tire of the airstairs truck and blowing it out.

Lux steadied his breathing, trying not to let the adrenaline rush of success send his aim askew, and pointed the crosshairs over the rear tire of the plodding vehicle. When he placed his finger on the trigger, a bullet circle appeared through the lens, shrinking with his pulse.

Aside from firing unassisted without a line, the only time a bullet line would be invisible with regular shooting was the first shot, when the target didn't know where you were. So at this point, SHINC could see Lux's bullet line from the airstairs. They'd be shooting back at him with machine guns or that antitank rifle any moment now.

But Lux triumphed over his urge to run away, aimed the circle—which wasn't quite at the center of his crosshairs—over the tire, and pulled the trigger when it had shrunk to its smallest size.

Getting the knack of the timing required the kind of reaction speed demanded by rhythm games. Lux had plenty of practice, and he did not miss.

Another gunshot. A golden cartridge flew through the air.

The bullet hit the pair of parallel tires in the rear. He spotted the fragments of rubber flying loose as they burst.

"Yes! Nice shooting. Now let's watch," said David, who was situated a hundred yards to the south.

The truck, now running on two flat tires on one side, began to list toward that direction. It turned left from its original route and started curving toward them.

"Leader, I can aim at the front right tire soon. Shouldn't we immobilize it entirely?" Lux asked, but David didn't answer him.

Instead, he wondered aloud, "Why aren't they shooting back…? Why is there no response at all…?"

And then he hit upon a theory.

"Jake!"

"Yeah, boss?"

"Shoot that truck about a hundred times or so. Doesn't have to actually strike it."

"You got it!"

Thirty feet away from David, Jake began firing his HK21,

steadied against the ground with the muzzle pointing through a hole in the chain-link fence. It spat fully automatic rounds at the airstairs truck.

A machine gun wasn't going to be as accurate as a sniper rifle, but with as many bullets as it fired, and with a target this big, some were bound to hit. The bullets smacked the truck and stairs at the speed of sound, sending up flashes of yellow sparks.

But the truck just kept trundling along. No one shot back at them.

"Aw, dammit! I should have known! They got us! Jake, hold your fire!" David swore, ordering them to stand down. The roar of the machine gun came to an abrupt halt.

As his teammates listened for the answer, David announced, "Well, gang, the Amazons really got one over on us. The truck's empty."

Bold watched the airstairs truck approach to a distance of about four hundred yards. With his eyes pressed to the binoculars, he reported, "It's true! The barrel on the top of the stairs is just a spare barrel sitting there..."

Even without intact tires on its left side, the truck slowly rolled onward toward MMTM. If they let it go, it would probably swing around toward the right again, carving a very lazy circle across the runway, until it eventually ran out of fuel.

"The Amazons probably escaped to the south or the center of the map by distracting us with this target to shoot at. They made us waste ten whole minutes doing this," David told them.

"Not bad," said Jake. "We'll have to thank them for this later." He exchanged the ammo box on the HK21.

Lux and Bold returned to the group from their spot a hundred yards to the north. It was 12:29. Four minutes had passed since they'd reached this area.

"I don't wanna play with the monsters, so let's move. We'll go through the airport, hugging the north boundary line. That way, we can check the scan as we go," said David. They all stood up and made their way through the fence.

Once through, they spread out to a mutual distance of a few dozen feet and, wary of the surroundings, slowly walked across the asphalt.

They were going north. Much like Llenn's group, they'd decided that if they moved along the northernmost edge of the arena, the enemy couldn't ambush them. That also meant there was no escape from an advancing squad, so this was a tactic only advised for teams with the firepower and fortitude to stand their ground and fight.

After a little while, Summon asked, "What about the airstairs truck, Leader?"

"Guess I could blow it up. The rest of you, get ready to check the scanner."

It had flat tires, but that wasn't stopping the truck from running. They didn't need another squad using it after they abandoned the vehicle. So David decided to destroy it instead.

It was about a thousand feet from MMTM to the airstairs truck at the moment—within his grenade launcher's range. If he didn't act now, it was going to drift farther away.

David stopped and aimed the Steyr STM-556 on a diagonal. He could puncture the fuel tank, but there was an easier method to doing it.

He grabbed the extended magazine as though it were the gun's grip, then rested his finger against the trigger of the grenade launcher below the barrel. When the bullet circle appeared for him, he placed it over the ground in front of the truck's path.

The time was 12:29:55.

The airstairs truck exploded.

A blue-white surge billowed around it, reducing the vehicle and its steps to dust as a huge azure orb swallowed them whole.

"What the—?! Get down!"

David removed his finger from the grenade launcher just before he was about to fire it and practically kissed the tarmac. The others followed his lead a beat later.

The blue explosion rattled their eardrums with a tremendous boom.

"Hya!" "Dwoah!" "Ooh!" "Gaaah!" "Hyeep!"

A number of additional spheres appeared, overlapping like bubbles and spreading. The entire diameter of the blast grew to over fifty yards.

It obliterated the airstairs truck, gashed a huge hole in the asphalt, and sprayed the chunks at the edges outward at the speed of sound. Those pieces shot toward the players like bullets, cracking the air over MMTM's heads in succession, even at a distance of a thousand feet. A few of them struck the ground, twanging off the ground like ricocheting bullets.

A few seconds after the blue explosion had finished and the flying bits of rubble had settled, David glanced up into the left corner of his vision at the hit point bars for his entire team.

"Everyone's all right, then..."

Fortunately, none of them had taken an unlucky hit from a random chunk of asphalt.

The airstairs truck had been completely melted away by the plasma surge. There wasn't so much as a little chunk of it left. The ground at the center of the explosion had been scooped out into a hole about a hundred feet across.

On top of that, everywhere within a radius of 250 yards was littered with chunks of asphalt somewhere between the size of a fist and a head. A hit from one of those would be serious trouble. If they'd been fifty yards closer, they could have all been in mortal danger.

David growled, getting slowly to his feet. "Dammit... They packed all of their plasma grenades in there... From what I remember, the gorilla-woman had a bunch of grand grenades. The ones she gave to the pink shrimp in the last Squad Jam to split the cruise ship in half..."

He'd watched the entirety of SJ3's battle scenes in preparation, so he knew the armaments, gear, and combat styles of just about everyone who had appeared in the previous tournament.

Surprised, Jake said, "Are you serious? What a waste of a good weapon... Oh! It's because they get refilled..."

"That's right. They got one over on us... The special rule refills their ammo, and the trap worked on us because they knew we wouldn't run from a fight. Shit!" David swore, his avatar's handsome face seething with fury. "And now they'll have all their plasma grenades back. But..."

"But?"

"They also know we're still alive. It's too early to be laughing, Eva."

It was thirty seconds past 12:30.

The third scan was already running.

CHAPTER 8

Girls in Peril

SECT.8

CHAPTER 8
Girls in Peril

It was an airplane graveyard.

A parking lot sat in the southwest corner of the spacious airport. Like the runway, it was covered in asphalt, but this was just an empty space for parking vehicles, a vast flat field of dark gray.

Atop it was an assortment of over a dozen business jets that would cost multiple billions of yen—the kind the very wealthy used for their own travel. They were tightly piled up in a space that was maybe a hundred feet in radius.

Some of their wheels were broken. Others were flipped over. Some were cut cleanly into two for whatever reason. Their paint was faded and flaking, most of their windows had fallen out or broken, and even the pilot seats were coming undone.

There were many usable vehicles in Squad Jam, but these didn't seem to fit the bill. Not that anyone in SHINC had the skill, either in the game or in real life, to fly a plane.

Everything was open around it, but the broken planes formed a little hill of cover about thirty feet tall, like a giant's toy box had been upturned onto the asphalt. It was the perfect place to hide.

That was exactly what SHINC was doing, huddled up like mice.

"Hmm. I should have expected it wouldn't be that easy. This is MMTM, after all," they muttered, watching the third scan proceed.

*   *   *

Ten minutes earlier, they'd decided to turn the airstairs truck into a time bomb. It was a little present—just for MMTM.

The mechanism to make the vehicle drive on its own was quite simple. First, SHINC duct-taped a few plasma grenades to the bottom of the steering wheel. That ensured that if the wheel turned at all, the weight would pull it back to an even keel.

Then they stuck a large plasma grenade, the kind known as a "grand grenade," to the accelerator pedal. Finally, to make sure it didn't go too fast, they stuck a belt of machine-gun ammo behind the pedal to prop it up.

All of these ideas came from Tohma, who had real-life driving experience.

The gun barrel on the top of the stairs was merely a spare PKM barrel placed in a likely location. They'd be losing that permanently, unlike the ammo, but it wasn't that expensive a part, so they sacrificed it for the sake of the trap.

They set the timers on the plasma grenades to go off between fifty-five and fifty-nine seconds after the clock hit 12:29. Once one went off, it would blow up all of them, but they were thorough—better safe than sorry.

Once their unmanned, slow-moving airstairs truck was complete, SHINC went sprinting as fast as they could to the southwest.

They knew from the scan that no lights had been at the airport, but that didn't rule out the possibility of enemies in wait, particularly troublesome snipers in the control tower, with their team leader located elsewhere as a feint.

That control tower, which stood at least three hundred feet tall, was going to be trouble. If someone took up a perch in there, everything within half a mile was in danger, in a full 360 degrees.

SHINC ran carefully, ready to instantly hide and counterattack if anyone in their group got shot. They made their way under the large rusted passenger planes sidled up next to the jet bridges, until they found their current location and took shelter, watching carefully for booby traps.

Not a single bullet was fired at them in the meantime.

"Now…where is my timeless rival, Llenn? I sure hope she hasn't died already."

Boss enlarged the southeast part of the map on her device's screen and tapped the dot on the bridge right before the wetlands. As she suspected, the name LPFM appeared.

"Wah-ha-ha-ha!" she chuckled eerily. It probably would have sounded a lot cuter from the real-life teenager Saki Nitobe. "There we go, there we go! You're finally coming out of the forest!"

Boss was truly elated. If Llenn's team chose to stay cooped up in that area to the final stage of the game, it would have presented a major challenge to SHINC.

Llenn and Pitohui had a strong instinct to fight, but M was their team leader, and he was cool and rational. Boss had been afraid he would choose the safest and most secure strategy.

"I think we'll get to have a real match this time…"

She was delighted at the thought of fighting with Llenn, and she hoped Llenn felt the same way.

Next, she touched the dot of the enemy team at the leftmost bridge, opposite from Llenn's team, at the residential area. It was DOOM, a new team competing this time around.

"Hmm?"

They were on the move, fast enough that she could tell even on the scan; that was a sign they were riding something. And they were heading for the rightmost bridge.

In other words, they were preparing to attack Llenn's squad. It was fairly close to SHINC's current location, too, in fact, but at the speed they were going, there was no way they'd be catching up in time.

"So Llenn's next opponent is them… Well, don't die," Boss said, offering encouragement to her enemy. Which in this case, of course, was Llenn.

Judging that they wouldn't be entering combat with Llenn's

team in the next ten minutes, Boss and her squad checked on the status of the other surviving teams.

In the southwest part of the field map, ZEMAL was raising hell. The one shining light in the crater-pocked region down there belonged to them, and it was surrounded by gray dots. They were the only ones alive there now. They had utterly conquered it.

"Those machine gunners have really gotten good at this!" Boss exclaimed, honestly impressed.

Rosa, a machine gunner herself, lamented, "That ammo-feeding system they have isn't fair. Man…I want one."

She really felt like getting some new equipment, just ten days after seeing them at the playtest, but Rosa didn't have anywhere near enough money.

The plans for the backpack-loading system, which was capable of firing nearly a thousand bullets without stopping, as well as the high-precision new PKP Pecheneg were both available in stores. And she wanted them. Oh, how she wanted them.

Players could use real money in *GGO*, but the price was two digits beyond what a high schooler's allowance could afford.

"Channel that frustration into your bullets and blast the enemy with them!" advised Tanya.

As the special rule stated, all the ammo they expended dealing with the monsters came back in full. Normally, the empty magazines came back to players after the finish of Squad Jam, but this time all that ammunition was returned to their inventories—even the plasma grenades they'd used in their trap.

Boss's eyes followed the map up to the northwest sector. There were glowing points here and there amid the ruined city, six in all. None of the teams there were eliminated.

Of those six surviving teams, only two had names Boss recognized: TOMS and T-S. That was the speedy, lightweight team including the SJ3 betrayer Cole and Ervin's team of sci-fi armored troops, respectively.

The groups were free to hack at each other for now. Let them go on a killing frenzy. Even better, let them pursue a course of mutual destruction.

That left the majority of the remaining enemies to the upper left of the center of the map.

The highway interchange in the dead center looked like a four-leaf clover. To its northwest was a frozen lake. From SHINC's current location, it was about a mile and a half to the west, across the north-south highway.

It was hard to make out the white dots on the white map feature, but once zoomed in, you could make out six blips gathered together within a space of about 1 percent of a square mile.

That many dots collected so closely on a flat, frozen lake could not possibly indicate that a battle was playing out. They were clearly working together. The other gray icons surrounding them were the unfortunate victims of this collective.

"Well, well, looks like we got a league of friends over here. So we're doing *that* again... I'll read the names," Boss said. She jabbed at the dots with a broad finger and listed them off. "WEEI, V2HG, PORL, RGB, WNGL, SATOH... Nope, don't know 'em."

They were names she hadn't seen or heard of in the three previous Squad Jams, with the sole exception of RGB.

"I remember RGB. They were the optical-gun team that Fukaziroh beat in SJ2, and the one we beat first in SJ3," said Tohma. A well-placed shot from her Degtyaryov antitank rifle had split most of them in two.

Sharp-eyed Tanya grinned and said, "But they've got the advantage this time, don't they? With opticals, shooting down all those monsters would be easy-peasy!"

"True," said Boss. "That's why they were invited to the alliance, I bet. So they've found a place to shine. That means that allied group won't have to worry about moving. They can hang out on the lake, buying all the time they want."

"No fair. Is there any way to break the ice there? Then we could wipe them all out at once," Sophie wondered aloud.

"Maybe with the plasma grenades… But it'll probably only create a hole where the blast is. The whole lake's just too big," said Boss.

"What if we run a real heavy truck over it? You hear news from Russia all the time about ice strong enough for people to walk over but not for vehicles weighing many tons. Even if it doesn't break, sometimes the place they run over is weakened, though you might not see it," suggested Tohma.

This is where it helped to have Milana, who split her time between Russia and Japan. She was full of information the average Japanese person wouldn't know.

In extremely cold and large countries like Russia, it was common for frozen lakes and rivers to be used as roads, because in many cases, it was the quickest way to reach the destination. That also meant broken ice accidents were typical.

"A car, huh? So if we ran a heavy, empty truck like the last one down there, we might take them all out…," Boss murmured, right as the lengthy Satellite Scan came to a finish.

The results of the 12:30 scan were as follows:

Llenn's team was in the woods, near the easternmost bridge.

DOOM was at the other end of the bridge, valiantly preparing to attack them.

SHINC was in the southwest part of the airport. MMTM was on the north side of it.

ZEMAL was in the crater area in the southwest part of the map.

Six allied teams were clumped together atop the lake.

And six teams, including TOMS and T-S, were in the ruined city. Seventeen teams in all.

So what to do next…? Boss wondered as her teammates watched the horizon for activity.

Using the map information in her mind and her knowledge of the others' locations and capabilities, she would need to think of a plan for their next ten minutes—perhaps longer.

She didn't think they had the ability to defeat the entire allied group on their own, so they were going to ignore them. Instead, she wanted to fight Llenn as soon as possible, so they ought to move south or southeast.

Whatever was going to happen with DOOM, Llenn's squad would probably win. Then they would cross the bridge.

So SHINC would go toward the huge shopping mall, or perhaps into the residential area around it, to wait. Once the forty-minute scan came in, they would know each other's location and be able to engage in the long-awaited battle.

"Good!" she said, surprised at how cheery she sounded.

So far, SJ4 couldn't have gone better for them. They avoided battle with MMTM in a way that was sure to get them mocked later on, but that sacrifice of their honor had turned out to be the right choice.

"We'll move quickly. South. Pass through the airport, cross the freeway carefully, then hide in the mall or residential neighborhood. Same formation as always."

The rest of the team chimed back, and SHINC was soon on the move.

The audience in the bar watched as the Amazons slipped out of the mountain of airplane wreckage.

"Oh! So that's where they were hiding."

When the group rushed to the south, a person in the bar noted, "Ah, must be going to fight Llenn's team."

"I get it. Ever since SJ1, they seemed like rivals."

Led by the silver-haired one with the Bizon, SHINC rushed from the airplane parking area out to the taxiway, then crossed the runway. After twenty seconds of watching this, someone asked, "Isn't this weird? Why are they on the screen if all they're doing is moving?"

"Good point…"

"Yeah, that is kind of weird."

The action feed always picked the most dynamic battle happening at the moment to display from multiple angles. Right now, several monitors were showing T-S doing battle in the ruined city with an opponent known as BKA, whose team members were dressed up like post-apocalyptic warriors.

A shirtless man with rippling muscles was rushing up on the sci-fi soldiers, probably shouting "Hya-haaa!" and blasting them with a modified shotgun. Their armor deflected all the pellets.

So why were the screens also showing SHINC, who were simply running from one point to another?

"Ah! I got it!"

One of the viewers figured it out. A battle was about to begin.

Someone had SHINC in their sights.

Unfortunately for SHINC, they couldn't see the video feed, so they had no idea what was about to happen.

They were almost across the runway area, just five hundred yards from the highway that ran across the map from east to west. The fence that acted as a boundary between the two areas was visible to the naked eye now.

Running at the rear of the group's formation, Boss was shot in her right pectoral.

"Huh?" The impact knocked her backward, and she slid atop the asphalt. "I've been shot!"

Since she was bringing up the rear, she didn't forget to warn the rest of the members who were running ahead of her and might not otherwise notice.

The left edge of her vision showed that her hit points were dropping significantly. Boss was tough, and she wasn't going to die in one hit, but the location couldn't have been much worse. It would take at least half her health.

"*Gah!*" "*Aaah!*"

Then Tohma and Tanya shrieked at nearly the same moment.

Like Boss's gauge, theirs began to shrink as well. They'd been sniped.

"Everyone down!" Boss shouted and, ignoring her own situation, prayed that her teammates' HP wouldn't drop too far.

The bars went down through the yellow zone and into the red, where they stopped at last. Both players had maybe 10 percent left. Those shots had been devastating. In a matter of moments, half of SHINC was essentially neutralized.

"Shit!" Boss swore, cursing her lack of caution and luck.

There was an ambush nearby. Either a roving unit with their leader situated elsewhere or a group in a vehicle must have attacked them. But there wasn't any time to consider these things now.

"The bullet came from up ahead! The highway! I didn't hear the shot—they've got a silencer!" she announced, coming to that conclusion based on how she'd been hit. If they were watching for a line coming only from just ahead of them, that would make it easier to dodge the next one.

Flat on their faces, SHINC craned their necks to look ahead toward the highway. Doing so would make it easiest to spot the enemy while reducing their own profile as targets.

Boss's health was at 40 percent. She pulled out an emergency med kit and stuck it in her thigh at once. Her body glowed briefly, indicating that healing had begun. On the left, the gauges for her, Tohma, and Tanya started flashing, an indicator that they were currently healing.

Med kits were very inefficient items: They healed only 30 percent, and it took them three minutes to do so. And each combatant in Squad Jam received just three of them at the start of the event. There was no trading or using them on others.

Of course, these rules were there for a reason. If you could bring your own recovery items, then a richer player could buy a stockpile of the best possible kind and gain a major advantage.

A few seconds after SHINC dropped to the ground, there was a sudden blast. It sounded like thunder, and the ground even rumbled a little bit.

"An explosion...? But that was far off," Boss noted correctly.

Then she saw a mushroom cloud rising into the sky to the southeast.

That was Llenn's direction. They must've been in battle. But what was that explosion from?

Despite her curiosity, Boss couldn't stop to think about it now. They had to solve their own peril first.

"Still no sign of enemies on the highway!" Anna reported, aided by her scope.

"Should we bring out the fangs?" asked Sophie. She was asking if she should bring out the PTRD-41 antitank rifle.

Boss's answer was immediate.

"Do it."

"Gotcha."

Without sitting up, Sophie swiped with her left hand to call up her inventory. Right at the top of her list was the PTRD-41. She hit the button to bring it out.

Having it out in the open here would let them use it as soon as they spotted the enemy, of course. But even more important was that if Sophie was sniped and killed, her teammates could still use the gun in SJ4. If it was in her item storage when she died, it would return to the waiting area with her.

Twenty seconds had passed since the attack, but no more bullets were forthcoming. The shots came from quite a distance, so it had been one thing when they were standing and running, but they were much more difficult targets flat on the ground.

Sophie brought out the PTRD-41, a gun over six feet long that was nearly all barrel, like some kind of drying rod. "I'll stand up and be the bait! Just tell me when!" she said, volunteering for the most dangerous role.

Boss had no reason to argue. Once Sophie stood up and started moving, the enemy would surely aim at her. And once they could see the bullet line, they would know exactly where the sniper was firing from. Even if the player had enough skill to shoot without a line, the hit location and facing would be enough to give them a general idea.

Once she was certain the team was all concentrating in the direction ahead of them, Boss put the binoculars to her face and said, "Okay, go!"

"I'm off!"

Sophie stood up, fully expecting to get hit. It would be obvious that she was a decoy if she wasn't holding anything, so she picked up the PTRD-41 by the carrying handle and proceeded forward with it held at waist height. It looked like she was trying to get the antitank rifle into sniping position.

If she was unlucky enough to get shot and killed instantly, her body would remain in place as an indestructible object they could use as a shield.

But after most of a minute, Sophie called back, "They're not shooting!"

She'd been ambling to make a good target, but there was no response. Instead, there was a second giant explosion in the distance. Did they perform the initial sniping, then pull back and move away before their position was exposed? That was what SHINC concluded.

Just then, there was a little puff of black smoke from the freeway, followed by a dull, soft boom. It had to be the effect of an ordinary hand grenade or grenade launcher.

It was followed by distant gunfire. *Ta-ta-tam, ta-ta-ta-tam, ta-ta-ta-ta-ta-tam.*

The sound was quiet and rapid, like a small hand drum being beaten—an assault rifle's classic sound. The lighter sound indicated a 5.56 mm weapon, and the rhythm overlapped, so there were at least two of them.

The airport was flat. And the freeway was a paved surface, too, so it was flat. And they were lying flat on their faces. SHINC couldn't possibly see what was happening in the distance. They had only the sound to go on.

"Someone's shooting at our sniper friend from behind, I guess?" Boss speculated, unable to think of a different possibility.

Her watch said it was 12:34. It bothered her that neither team's location appeared on the earlier scan, but it was possible if they were both members separate from the team leader. Or perhaps using high-speed vehicles.

"You can duck, Sophie."

"Roger that. Should we make a run for it?"

Boss considered this idea. Three of the squad, including her, were too badly hurt to be much use in combat, since the next shot to hit even a limb could kill them.

Rushing toward the freeway to the south and taking out all the enemies that might be hiding there was too risky. They had no idea what they were up against in that department.

And if they wanted to run away to the west of the wide-open airport, that meant a likely confrontation with the allied team atop the frozen lake.

If they ran to the east, that raised the danger that the group currently shooting at the sniper might attack them next. That left the safest route as the airplane graveyard to the north, where they'd just been hiding. Going backward, farther away from Llenn.

Argh, dammit! Boss swore silently to keep her team from hearing her in a moment of weakness. No matter how bad a situation might be, a leader should never let her subordinates hear any statement that might lower morale.

"Let's pull back to the wreckage again! Run at full speed! Let's get ready!" she told her squad.

But when SHINC started to tense their arms and rise up off the ground, they saw something that made the situation even worse.

"Wh-what?!"

Five hundred yards ahead, a trio of Humvees broke through the fence running alongside the freeway.

They were the American military's squat, four-wheel-drive trucks, the ones MMTM and then Pitohui and crew used in SJ2. They were recognizable by their flat, boxed bodies, as though someone had slapped tires on a huge, dented box.

Like the ones in SJ2, these were the M1114 model, where the

ordinary Humvee body was outfitted with extra plating to be bulletproof. They could completely block any 7.62 mm rounds.

An armored turret rose from the roof of each vehicle. The last time, they were sand-yellow, for desert combat, but these ones had dark-green camo patterns, for woodland use.

The three vehicles were coming their way, snaking here and there as faint puffs of smoke rose from their mufflers.

"Enemy vehicles approaching! Three of them!" Boss's team heard Tohma shout. She was already running toward Sophie, likely so she could fire the PTRD-41 and do *some* kind of damage to the Humvees. It was the only gun they had that could make a difference.

But with the way the trucks were snaking back and forth, they wouldn't have time to shoot all of them. The enemy wasn't going to drive directly at them mindlessly.

If SHINC split up and even one of the vehicles escaped, their opponents had the whole spacious airport to run over the helpless squad.

How to minimize the team's overall damage? How to avoid being wiped out?

Boss came to her answer immediately.

"Me, Tohma, and Tanya will attack. Gather up, and the rest of you, run for it!"

She sensed her teammates gasping. You could do that sort of thing when you spent all your time together, offline and online. When they'd first joined the gymnastics club, they'd had terrible chemistry, but now they could practically read one another's minds.

"All right! I got 'em!" said Tanya, rushing toward Boss. She reached out, grasping with her empty hand like a child looking for a toy or candy.

"Yep," said Boss, handing Tanya what she was looking for: two grand grenades.

Next Tohma came rushing toward her. She, too, held a grand grenade in each hand.

Boss clutched the last two and gave her final order.

"Sophie, you're in charge of the team. Go get Llenn."

As she placed the PTRD-41 back into storage, Sophie sadly but firmly replied, "Got it!"

The clouds were thickening in the vast open sky, over three Humvees that slowly made their way toward SHINC at a speed of under twenty miles per hour. They weren't going all out, perhaps in an abundance of caution. They were no longer driving in a serpentine path to avoid an attack.

Boss stared them down. Though she couldn't see behind her, Rosa's group should be fleeing at top speed at this point.

But Boss and her two partners had no means of escape. Neither did they have the ability to shoot their foes. They *did* have a means of blowing them up, however: the grand grenades.

It was a plan that did not leave any room for survival. If even one truck made it through, it could catch up to the other three members and run them over from behind.

In that case, there was no point in trying to throw their explosives. To ensure the best possible chance, they would have to take down each vehicle from up close.

"One for each of us. Don't get greedy. I'll take the one in the middle," Boss said to the other two.

"I'll take the right! Don't worry—I'm good at this!" said Tanya.

"I'll have the left, then. I've never done it, but there's a first time for everything!" replied Tohma. They sounded eager for the challenge.

Their foes were two hundred yards away now, close enough to make out the features of the drivers.

The players on the other side of the bulletproof glass were men in typical *GGO*-future gear: dark-blue pants, dark-green jackets with protectors, green masks, and single-lens sunglasses on their faces.

There were two men in the center Humvee, and one each in the side vehicles.

Boss, Tanya, and Tohma lay down, waiting for the Humvees to come and run them over.

But they did not.

She was ready to kill—and die.

"Huhhhh?"

So when the Humvees came to a sudden, screeching halt, and a signal flare shot up from the roof, Boss was utterly stunned.

The brilliant orange flare shone against the reddish sky and began to descend with a deployed parachute.

"What...?"

"The...?"

Tanya and Tohma could only watch in disbelief, mouths hanging agape.

About a hundred yards separated them from the cars. It was too much distance for them to charge forward and finish the job before the Humvees could react.

While they were unable to fathom what this action meant, the next one was much more direct. An arm stuck out of one of the Humvees and waved a scrap of white cloth.

"Are you serious...?" Boss muttered.

A white flag was the universal sign of surrender, but that couldn't be true in this case. There was no reason for them to concede this way. So Boss took it as a sign that they had no desire to fight and that they only wanted to talk.

"Is it a trap?" wondered Tanya.

"I don't see why they'd need to do that when they already have the advantage," grunted Boss.

She got up to her feet and affixed her grand grenades to her belt. If you had an item called a "Plasma Grenade Holder," the grenades would stick to your belt wherever you put them, like magnets.

It was the kind of thing that was easy to use, and nearly ubiquitous among players, but it also had a downside: If you were getting shot, it was easy for one grenade to set off all the others and blow you up.

"We might as well go talk to them. The three of you, keep running," Boss said to the other half of the team as she began walking forward. Her Vintorez was in hand, and she wasn't taking any chances.

As she headed away, Tohma called out, "Don't die on your own if they challenge you. We're still with you, remember."

"I know."

"If they try to pick you up, don't go with them. You're too cute to resist," added Tanya.

"Okay. But if they invite me out to have as much *GGO* parfait as I can eat from a café in SBC Glocken, what then?"

"If you eat it without us, you'll have hell to pay," the other two said in perfect synchronization. That sounded serious.

"Okay."

Boss closed the distance of ninety yards and stood before one of the Humvees. From here, she could throw a grand grenade and hit the car. But her pride would not allow her to do that.

"Here I am. I'm the leader of Team SHINC, Eva."

Her voice carried to all the members of her team through the comm, as well as to the people inside the Humvee.

A man popped his head out of the turret, which was surrounded by armor plating but had no gun. His face was completely hidden behind a mask and sunglasses.

"Ah, I'm so glad that you came. Now we don't need to waste time with unnecessary fighting. I'd rather not have my entire vehicle exploded with a grand grenade," the man said. His tone was friendly, but it was clear from his position behind the bulletproof glass and from the assault rifle in his hands that he wasn't relaxing just yet.

Boss glanced at his weapon: an HK433.

That was a Heckler & Koch 5.56 mm gun. It was the primary small arm for the German military in the present day of 2026.

In *GGO*, the HK433 was the newest and toughest kind of assault rifle. This was Boss's first time seeing one.

Since it was still so rare, it commanded supreme prices. His gun also had an expensive silencer attached to the end of its barrel. That suggested this team was made of either *GGO* experts or extremely rich players, or perhaps both.

Without missing a beat and without a shred of humility, Boss replied, "Depending on your offer, I might be willing to rush up and give you a big hug."

"Wah-ha-ha! I'll pass on that. I'd prefer to give you a proper explanation with the main force. Can you get all six of you into the cars? The scan is close, and we might get monsters spawning," he said.

Boss glanced at her wrist. It was after 12:36. They couldn't afford to take their time.

When he mentioned a "main force," she understood that to mean that he was one of the allied teams atop the frozen lake. That's where they'd be taken if they went along. From there, they'd be given a choice: Join the alliance or die.

"I have one question first. Who sniped us?"

"Ah yes, the three snipers. We eliminated them. They were from a team called DOOM," the man explained. Boss considered the possibilities.

DOOM had gone rushing toward Llenn's team. They'd left snipers behind, and the rest had gone onto the bridge to fight Llenn, where they'd caused some kind of massive explosion. It all seemed plausible enough.

"Hmm... All right, then," Boss said, making up her mind.

✳   ✳   ✳

At 12:40, SHINC watched the fourth scan roll in from inside the Humvees.

At 12:39, they'd called a truce and loaded up into the three vehicles, two people each, to hear out this offer. Before that, they'd been told to put away all of their guns and grenades into their inventory space.

"I see. So you're disarming us, in a way," noted Boss with a piercing look.

"Nah. It's just that there's not a lot of space in here," said the man with a shrug.

Refusing wouldn't get them anywhere, so SHINC complied, setting away their long-range guns, pistols, grenades, and everything else into the translucent briefcase of pure data that was their inventory.

The masked drivers and rear-seated Amazons said nothing to one another. The vehicles moved in silence, a line of three that crossed the airport.

Boss, Tanya, and Tohma used their second emergency med kits at this time. Even after the second round, only Boss would have her hit points fully recovered. The other two would be at 70 percent, but after consideration, they chose to hold on to their remaining health recovery items for now, in case they got torn down again later. It wasn't an easy decision, though—they could easily get killed with one good shot at the moment.

The scan started soon after they began driving, so the Humvees stopped and waited atop the runway.

The man Boss had talked to earlier, who was the only one on his team speaking to SHINC, turned around in the passenger seat. "You don't want people knowing you're moving during the scan, right? So we'll stop for a bit."

"That's considerate of you. How very privileged we must be," said Boss sarcastically, but in truth, she was grateful. This would give her a chance to see the state of the game and, more important, Llenn.

Of course, if LPFM was wiped out, they weren't going to accept the offer. She'd kill the driver with her bare hands.

The fourth scan started from the north, displaying the location of the surviving squads.

Not much had changed in the last ten minutes. MMTM was on the north end of the airport, at the very north edge of the map.

There were no potential opponents anywhere near them, so they were probably bored at the moment.

Two teams in the ruins area had vanished. As SHINC had hoped ten minutes ago, TOMS and T-S had done the job of cleaning up. Well done—keep it up.

As usual, ZEMAL was still around. But it was curious that they hadn't moved even a bit from the center of the southwest quadrant. They were aggressive to a fault, so you'd expect them to go on the offensive. Why were they suddenly being strategic and cautious? Had they eaten something past its expiration date?

The six teams on the frozen lake hadn't changed location. With RGB there, they were powerful enough to ignore the threat of the monsters.

Four of the members were in the trucks right now, which meant they had left their leaders behind on the lake. That was very risky for a team to do; that they were proactive enough to do so spoke to their confidence.

Lastly, there was one more team.

"Ah, good!"

Llenn's squad was still alive atop the bridge.

DOOM's dot was gray in the middle of that bridge, so whatever those mysterious explosions were, Llenn's team won the battle. It was probably a piece of cake. They were no doubt humming and sharpening their claws, preparing for the next battle.

SHINC was located fairly close, but there was no way to head straight for them now. Boss gave up on that idea. She trusted that there would be more chances.

Fourteen teams remained. In only forty minutes, more than half of SJ4's participants were out. That was a very fast pace.

The scan finished quickly, too, and the Humvees resumed their ride. Boss glanced at the dashboard to see how they were doing on fuel. The meter, which was placed in a highly visible spot, unlike in the real-life Humvee this one was based on, was shockingly almost at a full tank. They could drive for quite a while still.

I bet I know what it is, Boss thought. *There were more than three Humvees. They just siphoned off the gas from the others to fill this one.*

With a fuel tank and a hose, plus the Fuel Transfer skill, a player could simply pull those items out and hold them next to a vehicle, then move the gas to another one.

They could also do it the hard way, of course, by someone putting the hose in their mouth and sucking up the fuel, but like in real life, having gasoline in your mouth was a bad move.

The three Humvees rolled across the airport, huge tires trundling along until they reached the edge of the freeway that ran from north to south. A barbed wire fence with a gap in it about as tall as a person stood in their way, but the Humvees easily smashed the fence aside, and their large tires and tall suspension made it easy to roll through the moat.

From there, they crossed the vast freeway and drove off one of the exits at the four-leaf clover interchange, onto a surface street that ran parallel to the freeway. From the lakeside road going north-south, they could see a pure-white surface.

Tohma was in the same Humvee as Boss. "This is a familiar sight," she murmured.

The man in the passenger seat glanced at her curiously, but there was no way he could know she was a teenager from Russia.

They traveled north on the road for most of a mile, until another path curved to the left toward the gravel lakeside. The Humvee didn't stop there but rode straight over the ice.

Uneasy, Boss asked the man, "Hey, is this safe?"

"Hmm? What do you mean?" he asked, totally unguarded.

So she decided to play dumb about the safety of the ice and lied, "Just rolling us out in a totally visible area like this?"

"Oh, that? We're fine. Only friends around this area. There, you can see them now," he said, pointing at the white horizon, where little black dots were coming into view. They were about a half mile away.

"Ah, I see. That's good," Boss said, leaving it at that.

Internally, however, she wondered. If the ice beneath them cracked and gave way, she would die, but the allied team would die, too. Would Llenn be sad? Or would she be happy that triumph was that much closer?

The answer proved elusive. The Humvees roared across the ice at high speed, and they reached the group of six squads without any incidents of broken ice.

A little over a mile away from the shore, smack in the middle of the lake, an impromptu defensive formation was in place.

The little sesame seeds grew larger until it became clear they were people. They were sitting or lying on the ice in a big circle about a hundred feet across. The Humvees stopped about thirty feet away.

"You can get out now, but I'd appreciate if you didn't try any funny business. We'll have a lock on your backs at all times. I'd hate to have to destroy the team we already spared," the man said.

"Would a kiss count as funny business? Well, I'm sorry to tell you that we're only here to talk," Boss replied. She was joking around, but she knew full well that if she tried to pull her weapons out of storage, steal one of their weapons, or even attack bare-handed, she'd find a bullet in the back of the head.

Despite her nerves, Boss did her best not to let it show on her face. The squad regrouped and formed a line.

They slowly approached the circular formation. Boss didn't turn back, but she could feel keenly that there were sights on her back. It was as though the bullet lines cast off a heat of their own. Her teammates could surely see the line on the back of her head as she walked.

Does this count as being in peril? she wondered. She had no answer.

The closer they got, the more she could make out the allied teams' appearances. Sure enough, the members of RGB were there in the outer part of the circle, all alive, optical guns at the ready.

They'd fought in SJ3, so Boss remembered some of their faces. They proudly brandished their optical guns. Then one person with a machine gun looked their way. It was quite a hostile glare and very easy to parse.

"Hiya! Nice to see you well!" She beamed.

"..."

The other person pointedly ignored her. Perhaps he was afraid.

They passed through the line of guards and approached the men at the center of the circle. There were no women present, it seemed. Even Boss might get some positive attention here.

The men were seated lazily on the ice, some of them actually lying down. They were utterly carefree in the middle of such a tense battle-royale setting.

She didn't know any of the team names aside from RGB, so all of these people were new to the event. Their outfits were the same, so they had to be a team, she assumed.

There were two masked men with armored jackets like the men in the Humvees. That meant the team still had all six members alive.

I need to be wary of them, Boss decided.

Three men wore a toxic-looking camo pattern she'd never seen before. They were the only ones, so perhaps they'd been halved in combat. Or else the rest of the team was somewhere else now. They, too, were sporting masks and shades.

Watch out for them, too.

Then there were the men in tracksuits. It was a classic look: dark-blue suits with three white lines along the sides. There were six of them, all in masks and sunglasses.

Why are they dressed up for a sports competition? Boss had no idea why they chose the clothes they did.

It was almost like they had lost a bet and weren't allowed to wear regular combat gear. Of course, Llenn liked to wear pink all over, so there was precedent for this kind of sartorial choice.

SHINC hadn't seen their bizarre entrance to the pub, so witnessing the three squads all in masks and sunglasses stunned them. They made for a very suspicious sight—especially the tracksuits.

There were also six people in matching gray camo, and another six whose uniforms were a brown desert camo style. They weren't wearing masks, so she could make out their expressions. While they looked wary of SHINC, they also appeared somewhat proud.

You know you're *not the ones who are tough here, right?* Boss thought unnecessarily. She didn't say it out loud.

From what she could see, those six teams were made up entirely of men, thirty-three in total. As she approached, Boss tried to keep an eye on all of them, memorizing their body types and numbers.

Shit! Dammit, they're so thorough! she thought. Since playing *GGO*, her mouth had gotten much filthier. She needed to be careful that she didn't break into this kind of speech in real life.

Her spite came from the sight before her: None of them, aside from RGB, had their weapons out. Like SHINC, their armaments were all in their virtual inventory. They had nothing equipped.

That was not, of course, because they were showing to SHINC that they meant no harm. It was because they were hiding their true combat power.

Now there was no way to predict how they might fight.

But they almost certainly weren't going to be weak. With the three teams of matching masks and sunglasses on their side, the other two teams had to have pretty serious firepower to keep up.

On the flip side, they knew everything about SHINC. Anyone would know about them if they watched earlier Squad Jam footage. They'd know all about their tactics and all about their guns.

Would it have been better just to die back there after all? Boss wondered, sighing. One of the men stood up and approached them.

He was a very tall man, even by *GGO* standards.

In fact, he looked even taller than M, which was saying something. But unlike M, this guy was slim and slender—not burly.

He stuck out like a sore thumb with his tracksuit, mask, and sunglasses, though.

Did he have no sense of aesthetics when choosing this uniform? Didn't anyone on the team protest? And where could you actually get tracksuits in *GGO*?

Boss had many questions for the man, but the only one that actually crossed her lips as he approached was, "Are you the leader?"

She was a formidable character within *GGO*, but on the inside, she was a teenage girl. The situation had her quite nervous, but she played it cool to hide how she felt.

"Hi there. You don't need to be so nervous," he said kindly.

"So this is what you needed to prepare first?" Boss said, her own line at the ready. "Well, it's nice to make your acquaintance. I'm Eva."

She figured he wasn't going to tell her his name, but to her surprise, he politely and promptly replied, "Nice to meet you, Eva. I play under the name 'Fire.'"

Then he took off his sunglasses and mask, revealing a handsome avatar. "This is what I look like. Just so you know."

"Well…thank you. But when you're that tall, I don't think I'd mistake you for anyone else, regardless of what you're wearing."

"Ah-ha-ha-ha. That makes sense," he said, smiling pleasantly. Boss couldn't decide if he was being sincere or putting on an act. Regardless, she had a few guesses about the man named Fire.

He was clearly the leader of the three masked teams. Everyone started in random locations in Squad Jam, so it initially seemed like good luck that all three teams would have congregated without losing any members, but she figured out how they did it so quickly.

There was an unspoken rule that the toughest teams, like SHINC, got spread into the four corners of the map at the start. That meant a brand-new squad would automatically be much closer to the center of the map. As long as they decided that "no matter what map it is, we're heading for the center when the game starts," it shouldn't be too difficult to meet up quickly.

He'd certainly recruited some worthy players, probably with the power of cold, hard cash. Since you could convert real money into *GGO* credits, a rich enough player could easily hire BoB-level talent to his team.

And that wasn't a bad thing at all. It wasn't against the rules, and it wasn't even against the spirit of the game. Though it was a little infuriating for a teenage girl who had to scrape together the three-thousand-yen monthly subscription cost just to play. Scratch that—it was *super*-infuriating.

The three unmasked teams, including RGB, had probably been brought into the fold during SJ4. That was handily done, then—whatever it was that he used as bait.

"There! Northwest!" someone in RGB shouted at that moment. That told Boss it was time for the monsters to spawn.

Sure enough, shining polygons were appearing and concentrating in the northwest sky, taking the form of monsters. Those that SHINC had originally fought sported an animal theme, but these ones seemed to be machines. The first one to appear was a serving robot with caterpillar treads and scythes for hands.

"All right, folks! Take it away!" Fire commanded RGB.

With a crisp *shpow*, a Sorpressa A2 sniper rifle unleashed its energy beam. The unfortunate robot burst into pieces in midair without ever touching the ground. As it did so, it unleashed a warning cry to its fellows that was inaudible to human ears.

"Good grief. It's going to start the whole ruckus all over again. I was hoping we could relax and talk," said Fire.

"Then let's make it quick," Boss suggested. "We'd prefer to make our decision without taking too long."

Shpa-pa-pa-pa-pa-pow. Shpow. Bshoo-shoo-shoo-shoo! All around them, optical guns zapped and blasted.

None of the monsters seemed to be breaking up out of the ice. They materialized about three feet above the ice, a hundred yards away, and came charging once they touched down.

"Ha-ha! You came back to get wrecked, huh?"

"We'll smash 'em all!"

"Yaaah!"

RGB was ruthless with their gunfire. They were having the time of their life. At this rate, they were going to be too amped up to sleep tonight after having such a starring role in Squad Jam.

When she saw how quickly the mechanical monsters were dying, Boss decided it was safe for them to talk here. The rest of the team gazed in silence at the enemy squad they'd killed once before, now protecting their lives.

"Okay, let's get right into it. I want you to join our arrangement here. And I want you to follow our orders. We're trying to win this event," Fire explained. The optical guns continued to bark in the background.

"I'm not going to ask you 'What if we refuse?' In Squad Jam, you eliminate every team that gets in your way, especially if you're trying to win it all. So I'll ask the more important question: What do we stand to gain by joining you?"

"Ah, a very good question. As it happens, you stand to gain quite a lot. I think you'll be very happy," Fire boasted.

That caused Boss to raise an eyebrow. "Like what?"

"I'll create a situation in which you can fight the little pink one without any interruptions."

"…"

Boss was afraid her shock showed on her face, but if it did, Fire didn't react to it. He continued, "Llenn is the champion of SJ1 and SJ3. And I understand you view her as a rival, yes? You must want to have an all-out battle against her, like at the end of SJ1, and win this time."

What does it mean that he's describing this secondhand? Boss wondered, but she didn't say anything about it. Perhaps it was a slip of the tongue.

"Uh-oh, I suppose we're a little too straightforward," she said.

"Not at all. It's a virtue, young lady."

"I can't help but be pleased that you're calling me a young lady at this age."

"That's good to hear. Now, Llenn's team, LPFM, will be a very tough opponent. All of the other members are extremely power-ful. But if we don't beat them, we can't win the event," he said.

"True. But with this many people, you could probably take them," Boss said, gesturing toward them. RGB was still having fun with their target practice, and over twenty other men were relaxing in their circle atop the ice.

Fire replied, "I didn't think we could lose. But it also seemed like we wouldn't all make it. There would certainly be some casualties."

"Well, sure."

"And there are other threats around, like MMTM and ZEMAL. I wouldn't want them to hit us from behind while we're doing bat-tle with LPFM. I want to win, you see, but I also want to limit the team's damage as much as possible."

"Wait a second," interrupted Boss. Something was truly puz-zling her about this, and she had to ask. "You want to win it all. But this is a battle royale. In the end, you're going to have to fight your allied partners. What's your plan for that?"

"We'll all win."

"Huh?"

"Oh, it's not that mysterious. Once we've beaten the other teams, we'll huddle up close and use a grenade so that we all die together. Just like the third Bullet of Bullets. By default, every team will be made cochampion."

"..."

Boss was at a loss for words.

"I...never considered that...," she muttered.

Competition or not, the point was to fight. Who would ever come up with an idea like that...? She was partly annoyed, partly impressed...and partly annoyed again.

In real life, she'd been doing competitive gymnastics since childhood. The entire purpose was to battle for every last tenth of a point against other groups and individuals.

GGO was the same thing. It was a world of contests, where everyone played their hardest to win. She didn't understand this idea in Fire's head that everyone would stop and hold hands to cross the finish line together like best friends. It made no sense to her.

What if...he's not actually...trying to win the event...? Boss wondered, but she couldn't ask that. And it didn't really matter to her, either, so she let that idle thought sit.

Instead, she moved on. "Okay, I understand the logic. Getting to fight the little pink one isn't a bad deal at all. But what's your actual plan? Because I'm not going to play along if your only strategy is 'Okay, there you go—now fight.' We might just run away."

"I like your honesty. Of course I have an idea. I had plenty of time to think before you arrived," said Fire, flashing white teeth in a handsome smile. His eyes briefly darted to the upper right. "The next scan's...going to come too soon for our plan. It's nearly time."

He wasn't wearing a watch, so he had to look at the time readout in the corner of his vision instead. That sort of option was up to the player.

Boss looked at the watch on the inside of her left wrist. Nearly all *GGO* players preferred the wristwatch method over the utilitarian but boring way of checking your display. They liked to face it on the inside of their nondominant hand. That way you could see it while holding your gun.

Somehow, the time was already 12:49. Boss looked back at Fire, who continued his explanation.

"When we know LPFM's location on the scan, no matter where on the map they are, we will send you to their area. Our team will handle the perimeter security, so you worry only about your own fight. You could ignore our promise and run away if you want, but will you really do that? Once you've beaten LPFM, you'll be able to fight us for the championship. We'll be a worthy opponent."

"My goodness, what a tasty carrot you're dangling," Boss said, shrugging. She turned to look in the direction of her teammates, pretending to gaze into the distance. They looked back at her with absolute trust: *No matter what you choose, we'll follow you.*

A soldier values speed above all else. Boss made up her mind.

"All right. We're in."

The time was now 12:50.

Fire grinned and said, "I'm glad to hear it. Let's check out the scan."

"If you insist." Boss removed her Satellite Scan terminal.

The scan started from the east side. On the screen, Boss saw that Llenn's team was still perfectly alive on the bridge. She didn't know why they were taking so much time crossing it, but knowing them, they certainly had a logical reason for it.

Boss smirked and said, "If she's still alive, I can still kill her."

With RGB blasting away in the background and a swarm of monsters appearing and vanishing in a brilliant display of fireworks, the tall man smiled, his white teeth gleaming.

"I'm counting on you ladies."

"I know. Just leave that little pink one up to us," the gorilla-statured woman said with a grin.

The gust that blew across the frozen lake swung her braided pigtails.

As it blew over her, Boss thought, *I don't know what you think of us now, but after the next scan, we'll come to properly introduce ourselves before the fight.*

Llenn, don't die before then.

CHAPTER 9
Llenn's Fury

SECT.9

CHAPTER 9
Llenn's Fury

12:50.

The results of the fifth scan and the names of the surviving teams appeared on the huge monitor within the pub.

It scrolled across at a turtle's pace from west to east for the audience to watch. Boss's device started from the east, but perhaps for better drama, the audience was shown it from the west.

In the ruined city to the northwest, a fairly big battle had broken out and run its course. Two more teams had dropped out during the last ten minutes.

That left two survivors: the speedy TOMS and the well-armored T-S. They seemed to have been eliminating enemy squads separately, as they were well over a mile apart at this point.

"So the new teams are out... Well, that's no big surprise."

"You think those two will fight each other next? Or will they scamper off?"

There was no telling at this point.

Next, the scan revealed the bright, blazing dot of ZEMAL in the southwest area. It was strange that each of the dots was exactly the same as the others, and yet the letters *ZEMAL* next to it made it seem obnoxiously bright.

Their location was the same as ten minutes earlier. It seemed they were using the lip of the huge crater beside them as a defensive line.

"The machine gunners aren't moving, either... They're too chill."

"Yeah, what happened to their crazed charges? Do they have upset stomachs?"

"Let's just hope they haven't mistaken this event for a monster-killing high score tournament."

"Judging by the battle footage, it looks like that woman is taking the lead for them. She was doing a great job at it."

"Then that means..."

"Yeah, they're wary of that alliance at the lake. That's the biggest force going at the moment. Challenge them, and you're sure to lose. So they're waiting for their chance."

"Damn that hot chick... She's ruining everything!"

"How dare you turn ZEMAL into a proper team!"

The pub was full of righteous and misplaced anger.

Then the scan displayed the allied team atop the frozen lake. There had been six of them earlier.

"Are you serious?"

"What?!"

"No way!"

The crowd was shaken by what they saw.

And who could blame them? On top of the six teams from earlier, there was another in the mix, and it was none other than SHINC.

"Whoa, the Amazons went over to join the alliance!"

"That's crazy... It's not some game error, is it?"

"Nope, it's definitely true."

"Why? How come? Why would they do that?"

"Don't ask me!"

"Why not? She's your Eva, right?"

"She's not *mine*!"

On the screen, the scan continued eastward, providing no answers to their questions. There were two more teams left to display.

One was MMTM. They were at the northern edge of the

airport, having barely moved. Either because they were conserving their strength or because they were sulking about not having anyone to fight.

The other was LPFM. They were nearly at the end of the bridge. The scan moved onward, but there were no other teams to the east of that point.

"Twelve teams left…"

"That's about what I expected," the audience concluded. Then the discussion returned to the topic of the Amazons' mysterious choice.

Why would SHINC cease their solitary charge and decide to join the big team? Many opinions were offered and shared, but none of them knew the truth.

And while they didn't understand, some were angry about it.

Some in the game, in fact. Standing atop the bridge.

"Whyyyy?!" shrieked Llenn.

The squad moved across the bridge.

They were in the leftmost lane, right next to the railing. In the lead was M, large backpack reversed over his chest, a shield in each hand. To his right was Pitohui, who held two pieces of shield together. On the left was Fukaziroh, who held only one.

And in the rear, almost completely surrounded, a little pink shrimp screamed, "Whyyyy?!"

Why would SHINC choose to join the alliance when they were looking forward so much to a rematch? It didn't make sense. If anyone was *least* likely to team up, it seemed like Boss's group…

Llenn squeezed the Satellite Scanner so hard between her little hands that it creaked. They were indestructible items, but she was ready to crack it in half.

Fukaziroh glanced over at her and said, "Gee, I wonder why they did it. Even a brilliant bombshell like little old me couldn't tell ya."

M, ever calm and collected, proceeded forward slowly, wary

of snipers. "Nothing we can do about it. You've got to get over it and snap into shape. We're almost to the other side of the bridge. Once we can use the houses for cover, we run. I need you to be point again. Got that, Llenn?"

"Awww…"

"Did you hear me?"

"Uh… Once we're past the bridge, I'm point. Got it…"

Their twenty-minute sojourn across the bridge was finally coming to an end.

Instead of the team taking a quick crossing on the semi-trailer, they'd had to deal with suicide bombers on motorcycles, a betrayal from Shirley and Clarence, a horde of monsters, then a slow, painful trek on foot with shields up, wary of snipers. It had been quite an ordeal.

The residential neighborhood was up ahead. If they went north, they could cross the highway and get to the airport.

"But why?!" Llenn shouted again. She wasn't over it yet, not by a long shot.

Was there even a point to playing in SJ4 if she didn't get the chance to have a proper duel with SHINC? No, there wasn't.

"Why?!" she raged, as stormy as the Sea of Japan in winter.

"…"

M looked conflicted, but she couldn't see his face.

And neither could she see Pitohui, who was grinning. "Aw, Llenn, if you don't know now, you can ask them later, right? And the important thing is to survive until then! Am I wrong?"

"N-no, you're not *wrong*, but—!"

"Fighting with troubles weighing on your mind is a no-no! If you lack concentration and die in battle, you'll have to date Fire! You'll have to marry him!"

"Eugh! No— But— Wait! What? You said we'd just play dumb, like our lives depended on it!"

"Hmm? Did I?"

"You did! You said so, Pito! He won't have proof!"

"Then I guess I'll have to be his witness."

"No! Pito!"

"Ah-ha-ha-ha-ha! I'm just kidding. I think."

"What do you mean, you think...?"

"Look, my point is, let's go and kill the next enemy! You'll be able to take all that anger you're carrying and make it *their* problem."

"N-next enemy...?"

"M's going to explain for us," Pitohui said, delegating her responsibility.

"Yes," said M, accepting the mantle. "Our next opponent will be MMTM."

At that very moment, atop an airport runway over three miles to the north, David said, "Our next opponent will be the team with the pink pip-squeak and Pitohui."

"MMTM is far away, but they're the closest opponent if you disregard the alliance. There's nobody in between us. It's the perfect situation to fight them in the next ten or twenty minutes," M explained.

Meanwhile, David said to his team, "LPFM is the closest, aside from the alliance. Nobody else in between. It's a chance to have a good solid battle with a worthy foe!"

"Forget about SHINC for the time being, Llenn. If we don't survive a battle against MMTM, there won't be any chance of facing them after. Besides...," M said.

Elsewhere, David said, "Let's kick some ass, boys! It's time to go pay our respects to the pink shrimp and the lightsword chick!"

"Besides?" Llenn repeated, prompting M to continue.

"After we beat MMTM, we'll battle SHINC. Doesn't it remind you of SJ1, Llenn?"

"Ha-ha!" she laughed, causing Fukaziroh to turn.

The other girl saw a small pink creature baring its fangs, and a haiku came to her mind.

*I wish I could show
this terrifying visage
to the dummy Fire.*

"All right!" Llenn barked. "Let's go slaughter MMTM!"

"A little warm-up exercise for the newer, sleeker, four-man LPFM? You got it! And I'll be the one in the spotlight!" added Fukaziroh.

"Leave some of the prey to me! I'd prefer Daveed. He's the one with the ugliest face!" teased Pitohui, wearing her usual devilish grin.

"It's good to be motivated. But let me remind you, we're not going to recklessly run at a worthy opponent without any kind of plan or preparation," M cautioned, the voice of reason. It was as though he was saying, *This team is in big trouble if I don't keep it together.*

"Yeah," said Llenn, a little more composed but still feeling the magma surging through her body. "Plan time! Take it away, M!"

"All right. In that case…"

"First thing to do is search for a vehicle!" M said.

"First thing to do is search for a vehicle!" David said at the same time.

*   *   *

It was 12:55.

Once across the long, exposed bridge, Llenn and her three companions picked up speed—still wary of snipers—and hid inside a nearby house. From there, Llenn left and made use of her astonishing foot speed to rush toward the airport to the north.

Shirley watched her go through a glass lens. She pulled away from the scope and spat, "Ahhh, shit!"

Clarence, who was watching through binoculars, smiled and

said, "Ahhh, very clever! They don't leave any weaknesses open to exploit."

They were situated inside a church in the middle of the residential neighborhood. With all of the flat, one-story houses around, this was the biggest and tallest structure they could find.

The main wing of the church was a two-story structure built of white rock. A brick bell tower about twelve feet to a side rose from the top. The bell itself was located at approximately a four-story height.

The walls of the tower were filthy with age and covered by plants of a sickly color. At the top, a bell that once would have rung for young couples celebrating their marriages hung silent, never to toll again.

In real life, you could never bring guns into a place like this. But here, a sniper and her spotter set up on opposite sides of the bell.

A bit over twenty minutes earlier...

As a precondition to joining their team, Shirley and Clarence were promised by Pitohui that they could do whatever they liked once SJ4 started—even aim at their backs if they got the chance. Now they were acting on that promise.

Initially, they worked with the team to eliminate the monsters and cross the bridge, but once they got their chance, they took it.

They shot down the scout monster that appeared first, summoning the entire horde, then rode off on a motorcycle with the explosives the enemy team had used for their suicide run.

After their speedy escape on the motorcycle, they quickly found the church and decided to take up a position there. They moved fast to avoid being spotted by any other teams that might be watching.

They stashed their handy set of wheels by the dumpster around the back of the church, where they hid it under some of their spare ponchos.

There's one thing in common between idiots, smoke, and

snipers: They all love high places. That was because of the excellent visibility and shooting range, and the extra defense afforded by their advantageous angle, of course.

They climbed up the ladder into the bell tower, where they had a 360-degree view of the area. Despite the extra clouds gathering above, the view was spectacular.

To the north, the airport sat atop a vast parcel of land, with the control tower rising above it like a gravestone.

To the south, the large and quiet river reflected the sky. They could see the bridge they crossed to get here.

And to the west, the enormous indoor shopping mall loomed over everything like a squat fortress. In the distance beyond it, the frozen lake was like a pale board resting over the land.

It was rare to see such varied terrain all at once in *GGO*, because the extra data tended to bog down the system. This sight was a benefit of being on the special Squad Jam map.

The 12:50 scan happened, but their team leader wasn't with them, so they weren't in danger of showing up on the map. The leadership priority when they registered as LPFM was Llenn, Pitohui, Fukaziroh, M, Shirley, then Clarence. Unless the other four died first, Shirley and Clarence would be able to move undetected as swing members.

According to their readout, the distance from the church to the edge of the bridge was 564 meters. Strong wind or not, a target the size of a human being was still within Shirley's accuracy range.

Shirley had her gun's zero-in point at four hundred meters.

The zero-in point was a distance-tuning specification, meaning that if she pointed the crosshairs of her scope over a target, it would strike accurately if that target was four hundred meters away. That was assuming level altitude and no wind effects, of course.

You did this by first setting it so that it would hit at a hundred meters, a very close distance. Then you used the vertical adjustment settings of the crosshairs to move it up to four hundred.

If you were aiming farther than that, you had to consider how much gravity would pull on the bullet, and then you would move your shot upward accordingly. If you were training your weapon inside that number, you had to push it lower.

But how much do you adjust it, exactly?

There were excellent apps out there that would do the calculation for you, but if you didn't have the time, a marksman in real life would use their own gun and bullets at a firing range for practice.

How many centimeters below at a hundred meters?

How many centimeters below at two hundred meters?

How many centimeters above at five hundred meters?

How many centimeters above at eight hundred meters?

With painstaking care, you created your own chart with all the necessary adjustments and placed it on the side of the gunstock or inside the lid of the scope, where you could easily consult it. They called this tiny chart a "dope card."

But since she had plenty of time now, Shirley used a calculation app instead. She input that her distance would be 564 meters, plus a slight downward angle, and found that she needed to aim about 120 centimeters higher, or about four feet.

Therefore, if Pitohui showed herself on the end of the bridge, Shirley could aim about three heads above her target, and it should hit her torso. If she landed a hit on the torso, her deadly explosive rounds, which cost fifty times that of a normal bullet, would do the rest.

So in order to snipe Pitohui, and do it in one shot, they waited for their so-called teammates to finish eliminating the monsters and resume crossing the bridge—but of course, they weren't stupid enough to do that without a plan.

They defended themselves on three sides with M's shields, proceeding with caution. There would be no insta-kill in this state.

From time to time, Llenn slowed and fell out of her rear position, exposing herself outside her defensive position behind Fukaziroh's shield on the left wing.

Shirley had several chances to snipe Llenn if she wanted to, but she did not take them.

"Even though you hate her for killing you in SJ2?" Clarence asked.

"I don't shoot people out of personal hatred," said Shirley. She sounded so cool.

"Wait, is that a joke? You're chasing Pitohui around out of hatred."

"Pitohui isn't a person to me."

"Oh, you always have an answer for everything, Shirl. You're so cute like that."

"Should I shoot you first?"

"Don't scare me, Shirl! Anyway, hatred aside, it'd be easier later if you cut down on their numbers now."

"If you want to snipe her, go ahead."

"Okay! Let me see that gun."

"No. You'll break it."

Ultimately, the group finished crossing the bridge, and Pitohui snuck away into hiding.

Llenn rushed off for the airport and went completely out of sight.

Clarence slowly and deliberately turned herself around to look in the opposite direction, watching for enemies approaching from the west. Shirley and Clarence held a conversation, each looking a separate direction, in positions on either side of the bell.

"So what should we do now, Shirley? We know that Pito's trio is in that house there. Should we ride the motorcycle over and invade the building? That would be cool—like a movie scene!" said Clarence, offering her version of a "plan."

"You idiot. They'll hear us coming and completely obliterate us."

"But that's a cool way to die! In fact, let's use that suicide bomber backpack to do it!"

The backpack they stole from one of DOOM's dead bodies held

a terrifying amount of explosives, enough to destroy fifty yards in every direction. It was resting at the foot of the ladder leading up to the bell tower.

If they happened to get spotted by enemies and surrounded, and they knew there was no hope of victory, they could simply drop one plasma grenade over the side, set off the whole backpack, and blow up the church and themselves, with all the enemies included.

"It's one thing if we're dying, but I'm not taking part in any suicide attack while we're in a good position. Now think seriously."

"Okay. I'm good at that."

"..."

"Go on!"

"There are only two of us. Our goal is to take out Pitohui, but—"

"Not to win?"

"...That's *after* we beat Pitohui. Let's go over this again. Even as just a pair, we have two distinct advantages. Until the other four die, we won't show up on the Satellite Scan. I can snipe without a bullet line. And I have sure-kill explosive bullets. Correction: *three* advantages."

"And we're both beautiful. That's four. We can take advantage of all those poor sex-obsessed men out there. Why did they make it so you can't take off your underwear in *GGO*...? Those men would be helpless if we could flash our boobs!" Clarence ranted quite earnestly. Shirley ignored her.

"There's also one disadvantage we can't get rid of," she continued. "What is it?"

"Um, that we're *too* beautiful?"

"Take this seriously."

"Well, there are only two of us, so if a larger group approaches and surrounds us, we're kinda screwed."

"Good, you do understand. It means that when we're spotted, we're dead. So that requires great care in what we do. Don't forget that."

"Forget what?"

"Will you remember if I shoot you in the head?"

"Care! Caution! Roger that!"

"...If the three of them leave that building, we'll follow them at a distance."

"On our bike?"

"No, too much noise. On foot."

"Like a stalker," joked Clarence, but Shirley was serious.

"*Stalking* is what a hunter does to its prey. So yes, a sniper is a stalker. And I'm a hunter in real life. I've tracked several targets through the forest via footprints. When I get the chance, I'm eliminating Pitohui."

"Ah-ha-ha-ha. Got it. It's hunting season! And our prey is Pitohui. But...promise me one thing, Shirley. It's really important, and it'll have a huge influence on your public reputation."

"What's that?"

"If you bag yourself a Pitohui, just don't try to gut and skin her, okay?"

*　　　　*　　　　*

12:58.

"On the highway! Sector Two-Five on the map! I found something to ride!" Llenn announced.

Inside the house on standby, Pitohui, M, and Fukaziroh heard her voice through their in-ear comms.

When she said Sector 2-5, that indicated a portion of the map. Because the battlefield was measured exactly ten kilometers to a side, each of the one hundred square kilometers had its own code. From the northeast corner, she was talking about a spot two squares to the west, then five squares south. That was a notation system used in the board game shogi.

M set the map up in a hologram display on the floor, then zoomed in on Sector 2-5. This was the spot where the highway running east and west sent an exit lane off into its own road toward the airport.

Llenn's report continued warily. "What is that…? There's a big container here, with six weird-looking vehicles inside."

"Well, 'weird' doesn't help us much, Llenn. Can you use some proper vocabulary words?" Fukaziroh prompted.

"Um, they're motorcycles…? No. Unless…they are? Or maybe they're snowmobiles? But they have tires…"

Her description was lacking in detail. That left the rest of the team in the dark, but she didn't know that much about machinery, so it was the best she could do. The vehicles might be booby-trapped, so she couldn't get too close for a better look, either. And a picture was worth a thousand words.

"All right, we'll catch up to you. Stick to the container and stay on guard. Check the scan when it comes in. We need to be careful of Shirley sniping us."

"Roger!"

The three of them held two pieces of shield each and sprinted out of the protection of the house. Like Llenn minutes earlier, they were headed north.

"Okay. We're going."

"Yessir. Begin stalking!"

Shirley and Clarence joined them in taking action.

Hunters—waiting for their chance to strike from behind.

At 1:00, the sixth Satellite Scan started, and with it, ammo was refilled for the second time.

A message stating as much appeared before each player's eyes, but Cole from TOMS was on the run and didn't need that unnecessary information blocking his view.

"Dammit!"

He was all alone, sprinting desperately with his Heckler &

Koch MP7A1 in his hands. All of the teammate HP bars in the upper left were crossed out.

Cole was hurtling through the ruined city in the northwest of the map, with tall buildings standing or collapsed all around him. He stomped over a pile of rubble, leaving footprints on the roof of a burned car and kicking a fallen sign out of the way.

He wore a lightweight outfit of trekking shoes, leggings, shorts, and a simple utility vest with four magazine pouches on it. Like Llenn's, his character was designed to move quickly and cause trouble for potential foes. Therefore, he could only carry light guns, and he had little damage resistance.

As Cole raced through the torn-down city, too desperate to stop and watch the results of the scan, a grenade launcher's bullet line chased after him from behind. The looping line wavered in front of him, probably by coincidence, but he shouted, "Oh crap!" and came to a screeching halt before leaping through the door of the nearest building.

Kaboom! The grenade blast rumbled the entire area, belching up flames and smoke, then a little dust storm that occluded vision. It had been a close one; if he'd kept running, it would have blown him up for certain.

"Dammit! I'm not going to give up!" Cole ranted, determined to the last.

The "cheap" team on his heels was T-S. Their heavy armor stopped most attacks, allowing them to simply steamroller their opponents. It was a heretical concept to TOMS, whose entire philosophy was grace and skill: "Float like a butterfly, sting like a bee." It was the furthest you could get from their strategy.

And his entire team had been wiped out by them, leaving him to run away. It really sucked.

But Cole wasn't the kind of idiot who would throw himself into certain death against an unbeatable enemy anyway. He ran and ran for his life, looking for momentary safety.

When the smoke had cleared a little bit, Cole started running again. The grenade blast had just been shot at random and only landed close to him by luck, clearly. He was fast enough that he'd escaped their view, clearly. Clearly.

He hadn't expected T-S to be armed with grenade launchers this time. Like others, they'd been playing lots of *GGO* and outfitting themselves with better and better equipment, apparently.

From the squat, abbreviated silhouette, he was certain it was a Heckler & Koch M320. That was a single-shot grenade launcher that could be attached to a rifle, or snapped to a stock and used independently. T-S was doing the latter.

Three of them had the launchers, and given the ammo refills, they were popping off the grenades with abandon. That was how most of Cole's squadmates died.

"Dammit! I want revenge, but I can't get it like this," he told himself as he ran. Now that he was alone, the only goal he had at the moment was to continue running and hiding. Then, after all the other teams had killed each other, he'd make one last desperate attack at the very, very end. If it ended up as a mutual kill, so be it.

On his legs alone, he knew he could escape from the slow and plodding T-S, but vehicles complicated that picture. There were places in the ruined city where fallen buildings blocked the street, so it had better hiding options than most places, but how long could he rely on that…?

Suddenly, Cole's vision opened up ahead. He'd reached the tracks. Two pairs of rails ran over the ground here.

"Uh-oh…"

He panicked briefly at being out in more open space but recovered and grinned. There was a diesel locomotive only a hundred yards away.

"That should still work! I can use it to escape into the forest at the south end of the map!" Cole decided, certain of his new plan.

The train would rush him down the rails. Why not enjoy the decadence of a one-man railway journey?

His destination was the forest. There was no place better for a single person to run and hide. If the canopy was heavy, it would even neutralize the threat of a grenade launcher raining down from above.

"I've still got luck on my side! Just you watch, guys! I'll guide this squad to victory!"

Cole sprinted the hundred yards to the engine, vaulted himself up the ladder on the rear of the cab, and promptly set off the hand grenade planted there, dying instantly.

Boss watched the 1:00 scan from atop the frozen lake.

"All right, we can do this!" she said to the masked man who came to be their driver.

"No, it won't work. I'd suggest not," the man replied.

The scan revealed Llenn's location to be atop the highway leading to the airport. From here, it was two and a half miles there in a direct line. Traveling along the road, it would be more like three and a half.

"Why not?" Boss asked. She had no idea why the man would be so hesitant to drive them now. The Humvee could get them there in five minutes. That could put them close enough that each side recognized the other's location at the 1:10 scan, and they could have their long-awaited duel. And MMTM hadn't moved from the north end of the airport, so the likelihood of an interruption was low.

"Hmm…"

The man's face twisted enough that you could tell, even through the mask. He folded his arms, thought for a few dozen seconds, then glanced back at Fire, who was sitting nonchalantly in the middle of the circle.

"Well, I guess I could let you know. You *are* on our side now," he said, unfolding his arms. "The place where LPFM is now was our starting location. There are vehicles there. When the teams are placed densely at the start, we didn't want to stick out by moving too much, so we left them where they were. But if they're at that spot, they've probably found them. We left a present or two, but they're not stupid enough to fall for it, I'm sure."

"My goodness," said Boss. She got the picture now. Whatever the vehicles were, they'd provide major movement speed to LPFM, which could quite possibly leave SHINC chasing after their dust instead. This man surely wanted to avoid being caught in a strange spot during the next scan, too.

"All right," she said. "We'll wait for the next scan, then. Thanks for clueing me in."

"Oh, you're welcome."

"Now, if you don't mind, what *is* it that's over there?"

"They're weird."

"These things are *weird*!" Fukaziroh shouted.

It was 1:04. Four members of LPFM stood before the vehicles that Llenn found. It took plodding M's full running speed to get there this soon. In the meantime, Llenn had rushed around here and there, worried the monsters might appear if she waited in the same place for too long.

Two big metal boxes—shipping containers—sat in the middle of the highway. Right in the way of traffic. What a bother.

Containers had a series of unified international sizes, of course, and these were forty-footers. They stood about eight and a half feet tall.

Their doors were already open on either end, making the containers more like darkened tunnels. Both of them were packed with vehicles.

And they were very strange.

From a glance at their rear, they looked like motorcycles. There was a rear wheel, a seat to straddle, and handlebars that extended to the sides.

But seen from the other end of the container, where the fronts pointed, they had *two* wheels. The two wheels were spread to the sides, with a large body in between.

They were about eight feet long. The widest part of the machines was the front wheels, where it was five feet across. They weren't very tall, just three feet or so. The whole effect was rather squat.

Llenn had seen snowmobiles at ski resorts before; this struck her as what would happen if you stuck tires on one. Those ones had two skis in the front and caterpillar treads in the back, instead.

The three women were taking shelter behind the shield and keeping an eye out, while M carefully entered a container and checked for booby traps.

"What would you call these? What's their colloquial name?" Fukaziroh asked.

From the container, the team's foremost expert on vehicles replied, "They're trikes."

"Ohhh, *trikes*. Yeah, I know those," Fukaziroh said.

Llenn didn't recognize the name, so she was momentarily impressed by Fukaziroh's knowledge—but then it occurred to her that Fukaziroh *didn't* know, and this was only a setup for some silly comment, and she withdrew her respect.

"For it's one, two, three trikes, you're out at the old ball game, right?"

Llenn wanted to praise herself for recognizing it before it arrived.

M kindly ignored Fukaziroh's joke and continued, "*Trike* is short for *tricycle*. In other words, it's a three-wheeled motorcycle. I guess you'd define it as a vehicle with three wheels, with a seat the driver straddles, and handlebars instead of a steering wheel. Most of them have two wheels in the back, but some have the two in the front instead. Those are called a reverse trike. Some three-wheelers can tilt side to side the way motorcycles do, but they're just called three-wheel motorcycles, not trikes."

It all came unbidden to M's mind as if he was quoting straight from an encyclopedia.

"Ah, I get it," said Llenn, who wasn't sure that she did. But the real thing was right in front of her, so all she had to do was accept that "this is what a trike is."

GGO based its rideable vehicles on real ones, which meant these trikes were out there in the real world, and you could buy and ride one. She had no idea how much it would cost, though.

"Hang on—I stopped riding with training wheels years ago!" Fukaziroh complained. "So can we ride 'em?"

"Yeah, they're fine. Plenty of fuel. I disarmed all the nasty booby traps set up. So let's make the most of these six."

"There are that many?" Llenn asked, surprised. When she'd glanced into the containers, all she could tell was that there were a couple.

"Yep. Three in each one."

M pushed one of the trikes out into the open, hiding it around the east side of the container in case any enemies were watching on the west side. In the sunlight, the arrangement of two wheels in the front and one in the back was much clearer.

It still seemed large next to M, who was of considerable size. That was probably because of the sheer volume of the two parallel wheels in front. The body was a black-and-silver two-tone mix. It had that scuffed-up, well-used look that *GGO* vehicles so often did, but these weren't customized or decorated in a post-apocalyptic style like DOOM's motorcycles.

"Sweet! Then everyone gets one. Nice and easy! Should we hold back the last two for Clareley? Actually, never mind, no need to be nice to our deserters! Blow them up!" Fukaziroh cackled.

Llenn fixed her friend with narrowed eyes. "Do you really think I can drive one of these, Fuka?"

"Oops, sorry. Llenn can run on her own two feet. You're fast enough already, so you don't mind, do you?"

"How mean!"

"We only need two of them, M," said Pitohui from behind her shield. She was plopped down in a comfortable spot, protected from the threat of Shirley's sniper rifle by three whole plates.

"You and Fuka ride on one. I'll drive the other, with Llenn in the back. We'll ride them tandem."

Llenn felt relieved at the suggestion.

"Awww, I wanted to drive! I have my license, believe it or not!" Fukaziroh pouted. But when she saw the size of the vehicle before her, she retracted her protest. "Wait a second, my hands and feet won't reach!"

She'd been able to manage the gas pedal on the Humvee in SJ2—just barely—thanks to her large backpack, but it wasn't going to work this time.

M pushed out the second trike. This one was a different set of colors, splashed orange and wine red throughout.

"I pick this one! It's fancy," Fukaziroh decided.

Llenn didn't care about the color, so she didn't argue. In fact, there was a more pressing concern on her mind. "I'm sure we can cross the airport with these, M, but what about MMTM? If they're set up and waiting, they'll shoot us. We can't exactly drive holding the shields up, right? Though I'm sure that we could get away with the speed we'll have..."

Before M could answer, Pitohui said, "What do you want to do, Llenn? Avoid fighting with MMTM and take these to flee somewhere else?"

"No, I'll beat them! I want to beat them!"

"That's good to hear because I'm sure that Daveed wants to do the same. And..."

"And?"

"I'm sure they're looking for wheels, too—so they can fight *us*. To keep us from escaping. That's just a guess, but I'm sure I'm right."

"I see..."

Llenn thought back to the encounter with MMTM in SJ1, when they'd invaded with four hovercrafts.

Fukaziroh piped up, "I have a question for Miss Devious Pitohui."

"Go ahead, Fuka."

"You seem to know a lot about the mentality of MMTM's team leader. How come?"

"Well, of course. We were on the same squadron right after *GGO* launched. We've been through more than a few battles together."

"Ohhh," Fukaziroh and Llenn said in unison.

"And you see... Well, I suppose the statute of limitations is up by now. I'm only telling you this because I want you to understand your enemy better. The truth is, back then Daveed was in love with me! He actually did this weird pseudoproposal thing. He said, 'I don't care if it's just online, would you like to live with me?! I'll even let you call me Daveed!' You wouldn't believe it from the way he looks, but he was so purehearted! I mean, I turned him down, obviously!"

"Ooh!" Fukaziroh exclaimed—this time on her own.

"..."

It was a surprise to hear that the two of them had a shared past, but it also caused Llenn to remember that she, too, had received a proposal of sorts.

In a sense, her life—and also her gaming life—was riding on this match. Fire's two faces flashed across her eyelids when she closed them.

Llenn felt the resolve of a warrior hero welling up in her mind. *Any man who refuses to let me game...*must die.

She squeezed the P90 harder.

"That hurts, Llenn! You're cracking me!" she imagined P-chan saying.

In the driver's seat of an abandoned moving van they'd found on the highway running east to west, Shirley aimed her Blaser R93 Tactical 2. She had her bottom on the left-side driver's seat, with her back against the inside of the door and her legs stretched out across the right-side passenger's seat, the long rifle resting atop her knees. It wasn't the best shooting position.

Still, this was the only way to snipe without being seen by the enemy and without poking the barrel out of the passenger window.

Through her scope, about sixteen hundred feet away, she watched as Llenn's group stood by the trikes they'd pulled out of the containers. It was very easy to tell them apart individually.

"Ahhh, shit!"

In teams, the four of them quickly hopped atop two trikes and started to ride off.

M rode on one, with Fukaziroh straddling it in front of him. The other was under Pitohui's command, with Llenn over the back seat.

They raced north from the highway and vanished from her scope.

If she'd only gotten into sniping position ten seconds earlier, she might have had a clear shot at Pitohui as she emerged from behind the shipping container.

"..."

Shirley shook her head. She promptly engaged the safety on the R93 Tactical 2, slowly sat up from her unorthodox position, and got out of the driver's seat.

Next to the truck stood Clarence, watching out with her AR-57.

"Ahhh, no good, huh?" she said. The fact that Shirley hadn't fired told her everything she needed to know.

They got down and hid behind the truck on the east side. If anyone had been around, they'd have already been shot by now, but the two looked out for enemies all the same.

"They went north on two weird buggy-things. We're not gonna be able to catch them on foot," Shirley announced with frustration.

"Should we go back to get the motorcycle? Do you think there are extras of what they were riding?" Clarence asked.

Shirley thought it over for three seconds before shaking her head. "In either case, it'll make too much noise. There's a reason people don't use vehicles for stalking. And if they know we're there, we're screwed."

"Hmm. So we need something with no engine noise but that can move as fast as a car... Does that exist?" Clarence wondered. Shirley couldn't answer that question.

1:10.

"..."

Boss thought hard as she watched the Satellite Scan's results.

Two dots were moving quickly on the little screen in her hand. They were atop the vast runways of the airport. Right where her own team had started.

The two names on the dots were MMTM and LPFM. When the scan passed them, they did not stop moving.

It was like they were bragging that they had vehicles, broadcasting that to their opponents. And they were racing right for each other.

Good luck, Llenn. Don't die yet, Boss prayed to the unseen stars, blocked by a layer of gray clouds.

CHAPTER 10
Dogfight

SECT.10

CHAPTER 10
Dogfight

"Aaagh!"

Llenn nearly fell off several times.

The speedy black trike did not have a backrest on the rear seat. The taillight was right behind the edge of the cushion. Then it fell away, down to the cover over the wide rear tire.

Pitohui had played a number of VR games. She'd surely tried some of the driving ones that Fukaziroh was used to playing.

So it was no surprise that she had total mastery of this strange vehicle and was happily humming away as she drove it. She was very good at it—and very aggressive.

When they first started moving, the acceleration pushed Llenn's body backward, nearly throwing her off. As they continued onward, the centrifugal force did its best to hurl her away with each wild yank of the handlebars to avoid some obstacle on the road. It was easy for Pitohui; she just had to lean her body on the inside of the turn.

"Pito! Please tell me before you turn! I'm gonna fall off!"

"That's a lot to ask, actually. Do your best to hang on. You have to feel which way we're about to turn with your body. Your reaction speed is good enough, guaranteed. Oh, and don't grab on to me—it'll make it harder to steer. If you want to hug me, it's going to come with a kiss and a trip to bed, got that?"

"Ugh…"

She *would* do that.

Llenn gave up on getting help and used her free left hand to grab tight to the tandem bars on either side of the rear seat. That would be her only lifeline.

They were racing down the highway at a terrifying speed of nearly ninety miles an hour. The air around them was a buffeting gale.

To put it into more familiar terms with Japanese reporting on storms, the wind speed they were feeling was about ninety miles an hour. That was a typhoon-level speed, but those were usually measured in gust terms. This was a constant force.

The roaring against her ears was tremendous, and there would have been no way to hold a conversation without the comms in their ears.

"Hey, Llenn! If you fall off, you gotta run on your own two feet! Heh-heh-heh." Fukaziroh smirked from M's trike, which was racing along about a hundred feet away from them on a diagonal.

It was easy for her to be cocky. In addition to being large, M also had the shield-holding backpack, so they couldn't ride two seats like normal. Fukaziroh had to sit in front of him instead.

The handlebars were in front of her, and M's thick, rugged arms and thighs blocked her on the sides, so she was quite secure, with the ability to withstand both the acceleration and the horizontal g-force.

Because Fukaziroh's backpack was stuffed full of grenades and pressing against M's stomach, he had to sit farther back. Most of his butt was on the rear seat cushion.

This trike had the acceleration on the right handle, like a motorcycle, with a button on the left-hand side to shift semiautomatic gears, so there was no clutch or shift pedal. The brake pedal was on the right side, and it applied to all three tires.

According to M, these vehicles were supposed to have a cruise control feature that allowed you to set the acceleration at a fixed value so that you could drive hands-free, but the game wasn't modeling that feature here. It was either too dangerous or too convenient. In whatever case, the answer was a mystery.

Pitohui and M needed both hands to control the acceleration and gear changer, so it was basically impossible for them to perform accurate shooting, as it required two hands as well. If only they could, it would look awesome—like archers on horseback.

So Pitohui's rifle was resting before her, and M's was in a sling over his back. Naturally, only Llenn and Fukaziroh had the option of attacking while they rode, which meant they alone could look at the scan.

The terrifying high-speed rush finally subsided, and the two trikes made it to the airport. The road went straight into the inner part of the U-shaped terminal. There was a sizable aboveground garage in view. The route would eventually take them to the entrance to the departure and arrival lobbies.

But they weren't here to take a flight for a vacation, or pick up a returning friend or family member, so that was not their destination.

Instead, they turned off the road and drove through the busted gate in a brazen act of airport trespassing. This was a place that only airplanes should go—a stunningly wide and open stretch of flat ground and runways.

The few spots not covered by pavement revealed packed, dark earth, so really, they could drive the trikes anywhere they wanted. Nearly four square miles of flat space was theirs to traverse. The trikes were like little boats crossing the open sea.

The clock hit 1:10.

As the trike slowed to a slightly more manageable fifty miles an hour, Llenn slipped the P90 behind her back and used her now free hand to check her Satellite Scanner.

The allied team containing SHINC hadn't moved, so she ignored them for now and watched for the nearest foe.

"MMTM is moving! They're coming this way! North-northwest, a bit under two miles! Fast!"

"There we go! See, Daveed is so easy to understand!"

"How fast are they going, Llenn?" M asked, so Llenn zoomed in on the map until only the two of them were displayed. The dots' movement speed increased quite a bit, so she could tell the other one was just a tad faster.

"Faster than us!"

"Motorcycles?" M wondered.

"No, I bet they're using these. The same trikes," said Pitohui, patting the fuel tank with her left hand. "Too hard to shoot while riding a motorcycle. You have to tilt the body to turn, and if you lose balance, you wipe out. They wouldn't choose bikes to fight here. Neither would I. There were more trikes to the north. They got them way earlier than us and used them to shorten their movement distance without anyone noticing."

"I see…" "I see!" said Llenn and Fukaziroh in succession.

Pitohui turned the handlebars to the left a bit, pointing the trike toward MMTM. A moment later, M followed her lead.

"We're going to fight without stopping, got that? The instant you stop, you'll get surrounded and shot. We shoot at each other on the move. It's like an airplane dogfight. Are our gunners ready?"

With an MGL-140 in each hand, Fukaziroh immediately replied, "You bet!" like a hyped-up seller at a fish market. Their bulky round bodies rested atop the trike's fuel tank. Now the trike was a gunship with a pair of fore grenade cannons.

Llenn put the Satellite Scan terminal in her chest pocket, swung the P90 back around to her hands, and made sure that the safety switch was set to full auto.

"Whew. Ready!" she said to pump herself up, but her doubts still remained. "The problem is, I can hardly see around Pito, so I can't shoot forward…"

All she'd been looking at for the past few minutes was the combat vest on Pitohui's back, the pouch where she kept her lightswords, and the ponytail that kept smacking Llenn's nose as it whipped about in the wind.

This was an impossible situation for her to be the gunner. Fortunately, Pitohui was filled with benevolent advice.

"I know. Just turn yourself around and sit backward."

"Okay...... Wait, what?!"

"Hurry, hurry! They're about to come into view!"

"N-ngh..."

Reluctantly, Llenn released her left hand and grabbed Pitohui's back, then rose to a half-standing position over the seat. Her legs trembled with fear. If the trike took a hard turn now, she'd fly right off it.

Slowly and hesitantly, Llenn managed to turn her body until she was facing backward.

"Eep..."

Naturally, this brought a much greater field of view, as the scenery zoomed away from her.

Llenn was used to rushing around at high speeds on her own two feet, so background imagery rushing past her was nothing new. But seeing it happen in reverse was very new, and the novelty of it frightened her.

She'd had her feet on the tandem steps before, but with her body turned around, that was no longer possible. They had to dangle unsupported. She squeezed the seat with her thighs and held on tighter with her left hand.

Llenn was terrified at the notion of falling off. Since there was no seat belt here, she considered using a length of rope to tie her belt to Pitohui's, but then she realized, *No, that won't work. If I fall off, I'll get dragged as I become a bloody pulp...*

Llenn imagined herself clanging around on the ground along with a bunch of empty cans hanging from the bumper of a car with a sign reading JUST MARRIED! on the back. She decided it was better to fall off entirely than be dragged over asphalt until she died.

"Tallyho!" cried Fukaziroh. That was an old traditional call to indicate that prey had been sighted on a foxhunt, and it was used in a modern context by fighter pilots when they spotted an enemy.

Llenn was facing backward, so she couldn't see anything yet, but it was surely a sign that MMTM was visible on the horizon of the flat runway.

"They *are* on the same trikes. I see six," M helpfully added. MMTM was riding one person to a trike.

"I don't need to tell you, do I, M?"

"Nope. One strike and then withdraw. Fire each grenade carefully, Fuka. We don't have time for a steady reload. Shoot all twelve. We can't expect accuracy to the sides with lobbed grenades, so only shoot straight ahead."

"You got it! Straight ahead? I'm your gal! That's the only way I know how to live!"

"Llenn, you aim at anyone who tries to swing behind us. Don't skimp on the bullets."

"R-roger that!"

"And don't spend all your time regretfully looking behind you into the past, okay...?" Fukaziroh teased.

"This has nothing to do with my way of life! And I don't actually spend my time focused on the past!" Llenn snapped back at Fukaziroh. Then she remembered something more important, and she asked her teammates, "If they're each riding one to the same vehicles, won't they be faster than us...?"

Pitohui answered, "Yep. But they need to drive and shoot at the same time, so they'll be busier than us."

"I see..."

In her mind, Llenn tried to simulate an encounter between an enemy with greater numbers but less efficiency and their own squad, with fewer numbers but clearer roles for each person. It didn't give her any answers.

"So who has the advantage?" she blurted out.

"Who knows?! You gotta do it and see what happens! My guess is, the advantage goes to whoever fights to the end without giving up," said Pitohui optimistically.

"That makes sense! All right! Let's do this, P-chan!"

The audience watching from the pub stared at the aerial footage.

On the main monitor, formations of two and six vehicles were rapidly racing toward each other on a sea of asphalt. They were on opposite sides of the screen, so as they approached, the image zoomed in.

Six trikes, identical to the ones LPFM was riding, formed a horizontal line at an interval of about twenty yards each, covering the spacious grounds.

For now, the members of MMTM did not have weapons in hand. Their assault rifles, sniper rifles, and machine guns were hanging from slings and resting on their laps, and both hands were on the bars. They were focused on driving.

Not surprisingly, they'd found the trikes in shipping containers over ten minutes ago. That gave them a bit of time to practice riding them and get the feel of their handling. Then they waited, ready to hop on and rush any foes who ventured onto the airport.

David figured that if LPFM came for them, it would be on wheels, but he didn't expect the exact same trikes—or that it would just be two of them. He didn't know that LPFM was a six-person team this time—or that the other two had already run off on their own.

If their enemy had come in a truck or a 4WD vehicle, they could use the trikes' speed to circle around them, then stop and attack from long distance, resuming their movement when the enemy tried to fire back. Then another trike could approach from behind and repeat the attack pattern.

It would be like a pack of wolves taking down a large prey animal, attacking with waves as often as possible, which is why they chose one trike for each member.

But that wouldn't work if LPFM was on two trikes. Could they stop and attack to do enough damage to their current opponent? That was unlikely.

For one thing, LPFM had just as much space and mobility. They could easily zip away or zoom straight through any potential encirclement. *GGO*'s unique bullet-line system would make it easier for them.

That left only one real strategy: to keep up their own mobility and maintain the pressure of the chase.

When David realized that their advantage of numbers wasn't going to guarantee them tactical superiority, he grumbled internally, *Damn you, Pitohui.* It was surely that vixen's idea to limit their number rather than taking four trikes.

In fact, he wanted to put three bullets in his own head for ever having fallen in love with such a woman. Instead, he gave more orders to his team.

"We're going to blaze right past them! Don't chicken out and turn away! That'll only make it easier for them to pick you off!"

Since they were both rushing by each other at high speed, if someone turned sideways to dodge, that would expose their flank to the enemy's attack.

No matter how frightening it might be, once they passed each other, they'd just have to spin around to take the opponent's rear.

Once his teammates had responded, David barked, "Let's go! Time to hunt a poisonous bird!"

On the screen in the pub, two and six trikes approached at high speed.

Their relative velocity had to be over 150 miles per hour. This was a speed no one had ever seen in *GGO* before.

"It's like a jousting match... So what'll happen?"

"I dunno, but there is one thing I know—this interaction is gonna be over in the blink of an eye."

"Way to say the most obvious thing in the world as if it's some kind of revelation..."

"I'm just saying, don't blink."

There was no other battle happening, so all the monitors were displaying this interaction.

The bar fell silent.

As the two sides closed the gap at a rate of seventy-five yards a second, M's calm, careful voice said, "Fire one time, Fuka. You choose the target and timing. After we've passed, fire at will, Llenn."

"Roger that! I got it!"

"R-roger! Fuka, I'm counting on you!"

Fukaziroh grinned. "It's good to be relied on!"

In her right hand was the MGL-140 named Rightony. In her left was Leftania. Her tiny index fingers waited, barely keeping space from the triggers.

When they were four hundred yards apart, just seconds from colliding, Fukaziroh did not fire.

Three hundred yards. She did not fire.

Two hundred yards. Her index fingers touched the triggers, generating two bullet lines that pointed forward, then stretched until they were nearly horizontal...

"Ha-ha!"

When Kenta saw the line appear straight ahead, he turned the handlebars slightly to his right.

He anticipated that the grenade girl on LPFM would attempt to shoot at them before they passed. He spotted her sitting in front of M on the right trike about two seconds before this.

All he had to do was watch and avoid the bullet line. Unlike a bullet at Mach 2, a grenade flew much slower, so whether she shot it upward or straight ahead of her, he would be able to evade it without trouble, as long as he paid attention to the bullet line.

Kenta's trike changed directions, gliding to the right like it was changing lanes on the highway, and collided with Lux's trike to its right.

He saw his own face reflected in Lux's sunglasses.

When LPFM and MMTM passed each other, two of the trikes were already completely off the ground.

Kenta's and Lux's vehicles experienced a nasty sideswipe, and they shot away from each other on the rebound.

The trikes had a function to maintain stability and prevent drifting or rolling, but they weren't quite capable of stopping the force of a full collision.

Kenta's trike flipped over to the left, and Lux's to the right.

"Urgh!" "Hya!"

Both of them flew into the air. Kenta landed on his back, while Lux landed on his head. The vehicles smacked off the asphalt and continued to roll sideways.

LPFM and MMTM passed each other, now traveling *apart* at seventy-five yards a second.

"Hya-haaa!"

Llenn spotted the cause of Fukaziroh's delight at once.

Six trikes made their way into her field of vision from behind, with four of them rapidly speeding past. It was an incredibly brief encounter because, from the moment they appeared, they were already just dots in the distance.

The other two trikes appeared two seconds later, rolling and spinning. Parts of them broke off with each collision against the asphalt, wrecking the things. Amid the howling of the wind in her ears, she heard the crashing and smashing of machinery.

One of the riders slid on his back along the asphalt, damage coloration visible as the little polygonal effects splintered off.

The other one's head was tilted at an unnatural angle as he bounced and rolled through the air near his trike. The DEAD tag was already floating over his head. With each bounce against the ground, the limbs of the body jolted and flopped.

The long rifle on his back snapped in half. Sadly, the MSG90 he'd been using since SJ3 was likely trashed for good.

So stunned that she couldn't even fire the P90 once, Llenn asked, "Um...what just happened?"

She didn't hear Fukaziroh fire a single grenade, and yet two enemies were destroyed from the trikes passing, and one of them was dead.

"A little magic spell. That's all," said Fukaziroh.

"You tricky sylph. What did you really do?" asked Llenn, skeptical. Maybe if this were *ALfheim Online*, it would be magic.

"Oh, I just blinked my bullet line at a tricky time interval to either side of those two trikes! They panicked and swerved away, toward each other, until they bonked! You guys better drive safer than that in real life! Didn't you go to driving school? Always check your blind spots!"

"Whoa…you *are* a magician!" Llenn exclaimed.

"Way to go!" said Pitohui.

"Nice one," added M. Then he asked, "Llenn, I know one of them died. What about the other one?"

Llenn squinted to see what happened to the black-haired man who slid on the ground, but she couldn't make out the color of a DEAD tag from this distance.

"He took a lot of damage, but he should still be alive!"

"Got it."

"M, stop the vehicle for me. If there was an accident, they should be rushing over to pick him up. Shall I pop 'em with one?" Fukaziroh suggested.

"No. They're not that naïve," said M.

"Lux is dead! My HP is down to twenty percent… Sorry!" called out Kenta, who'd been thrown off his trike.

David made a snap decision. "Stay there and focus on healing! We'll get you later!"

"R-roger…"

"Form a vertical line after me! Right turn!"

The other four peeled off into a curve with David at the lead.

"We picked off one, but they're not going to let us get away after that. We're going to mount another head-on attack," announced M as he applied the brakes so he could safely turn.

Pitohui followed his lead and braked, but much harder. Llenn wasn't ready, and the sudden deceleration g-force smacked her head against the bulletproof armor on Pitohui's back.

"Ow!"

*   *   *

By the time their two trikes finished turning around counter-clockwise, David's squad was already pointed straight toward them—racing at full throttle.

Pitohui jammed on the accelerator, so this time Llenn's head lurched forward, nearly planting her down on the ground.

"Eeeeek!" she shrieked in terror.

If she fell, she'd wind up bouncing on the ground with a broken neck, like the dead man she'd just witnessed seconds earlier.

Traffic accidents are scary... Better try even harder to avoid them from now on, she decided. Between getting shot with a gun and being in a car crash, the latter was much more likely in real life.

It occurred to her that maybe forcing people who were guilty of reckless driving to experience a horrifying VR traffic accident might actually scare them into being more responsible.

"They're not going to pass straight by us this time. They'll probably split both ways before they reach us."

"How do ya know that, Pito?"

"Woman's intuition."

"Then it's as good as gold," replied Fukaziroh. In the mean-time, the distance between them and the enemy was rapidly shrinking again.

M told Fukaziroh, "Do it again. It's up to you."

"You got it!"

Pitohui told Llenn, "You attack this time, too, Llenn. It's all right. You're good at this. You'll get the hang of it."

"Huh? Of what?"

"You'll know once you do it."

Llenn didn't know what to think.

"Five seconds," said M in her ear. She clutched the P90.

When Fukaziroh saw that MMTM was spacing themselves out wider than before, she said, "Oh well!" and fired one shot each from Rightony and Leftania.

They were meant to land in front of the high-speed targets, but the four trikes split to the right and left with proper timing upon seeing the bullet lines. The grenades landed between them and exploded, doing nothing more than tearing up a tiny chunk of asphalt.

"Tch! No good! Llenn, they went to the sides!"

"G-got it!"

Llenn pressed the gun to her shoulder with just one hand and focused on the left side, which would be easier for her to aim at.

When a trike first crossed into her view, she pulled the trigger at once. The rapid succession of bullets was nearly one continuous sound without individual shots—a stream of lead erupted before her.

"Hrmm..."

Not one of them hit. They passed on the side less than a hundred feet away, which was very close, and the trikes were big targets, so Llenn figured that even without much in the way of marksmanship, she'd at least hit them once.

She understood why.

The bullet circle wasn't where she was training her weapon. She'd aimed ahead of the moving target to make sure it led the trike into her gunfire, but the expanding and contracting circle was far *behind* the mark instead.

"Oh...I get it!"

Like Pitohui had just warned her a moment ago, Llenn figured it out at once.

"Everyone's all right. Good. Then let's split into two pairs and do a wave attack! If you can go for it, go! Don't give them time to regroup or rest!" David ordered. MMTM swiftly braked and turned, then rushed back after LPFM's two trikes.

The most skilled driver, who cut a sharp left turn and raced full bore after his target, was Summon. The wind smacked at his cut body.

He rushed after Pitohui's vehicle from a position of about 250 feet to the right. The fore and aft distance between them was steadily closing.

Once he was at the trike's top gear, Summon let go with his

left hand so that he was driving with only the right in a feat of high-speed, one-handed control. The bike zoomed across the runway with utter precision and stability.

Next, with his free hand, he grabbed the FN Herstal SCAR-L assault rifle hanging around his shoulders. The stock was folded up, so he could hold it like a pistol.

With his preparations complete, Summon gunned the acceleration and pushed the handlebars to the left. Now he was zooming toward Pitohui's trike from the right.

It was the kind of strafing run that a fighter jet would do in an aerial battle, so he didn't have time to set up the bullet circle and aim with it. Summon used his own aim and hugged it to his side to steady the gun at full auto.

His target—Pitohui's trike—grew rapidly larger in his eyes.

"Gotcha!" he said and opened fire one-handed. With a great rattling sound, the weapon loosed a volley of bullets—and they all missed.

"Huh? What the—?"

So that's what it means!

The enemy's shooting confirmed what Llenn had guessed from her intuition earlier.

He came over on a slant from the right and aimed at them as he passed by, but his shots—which were too fast to see, so it was really his bullet lines—passed right by their trike, about thirty feet in front.

The bundle of bullet lines meant the shooting was steady and aimed, not a wild spray. He'd been trying to hit them exactly on target, but all of the shots wound up going somewhere completely different.

There could only be one reason for that. His *aim* was completely wrong.

But he had clearly done it properly and accurately. He shot with confidence because he knew that at this range, he couldn't possibly miss.

And yet he did, very cleanly, and just as Llenn had done a moment earlier.

She figured out why it happened.

It was because not only was the target moving at high speed, so was the shooter.

When you were stationary and the target was moving, you could simply aim ahead of the target's path. That wasn't very difficult to do; aiming ahead of a running opponent was something every *GGO* player had to learn to do consistently.

But when *you* were the one moving, everything was reversed.

If you were moving and the target was stationary, you would never hit them by aiming right at the target. The vector of the shooter's own movement—the speed and direction—would be added to the bullet, striking ahead of the target instead.

The enemy had rushed up and past them on a diagonal slant. Since he was faster than them, the bullets he shot rushed past them and went in front, passing them harmlessly.

"Pito, this is gonna be really hard to aim!" Llenn complained.

From the front seat came her answer. "Yeah, I bet. But you're used to it, right? And your partner is good at it, too, right?"

"Of course!" Llenn said energetically.

She'd pushed her agility as high as it could go, and she could move very fast on her own two feet. She had plenty of experience shooting and fighting while running that fast. And her P90 partner's fifteen-rounds-per-second rate of fire assisted that strategy.

"I'm used to the speed *and* to your violent driving!"

"That's what I like to hear, Llenn! So maybe we should quit playing nice and end this, eh? M, you two can sit back and sip some tea."

On the other trike, M said, "Got it."

"Awww, I only shot two grenades! Oh well. You can clean up the rest, Llenn!"

From the bar, the audience saw Pitohui's and M's trikes separate significantly. Confused by LPFM's strategy, someone wondered out loud, "What? Are they splitting up?"

"If they're trying to run away, will that even work? Riding two to a vehicle makes 'em slower, so they'll easily get caught."

"Yeah, for sure. What's up with that Pitohui chick? Has she run out of ideas?"

"Is this the end for Llenn?"

"Get 'em, skull team!" cheered the audience, who had no concept of loyalty. But when the trike with the tiny pink rider suddenly took a wide turn, they shouted, "No! They're gonna fight!"

"Awright, here we go!" Pitohui called out with delight.

"Yes! Gooo!" said Llenn. She squeezed with her left hand and her thighs.

Then the engine roared at a high pitch. The trike shot forward as though it had been kicked and began a right turn. The rear tire slid a little, causing the vehicle's control system to intercede and keep it rotating without drifting.

"Urrrrrgh!" Llenn groaned, resisting the force that threatened to hurl her off.

This experience taught her that, in fact, what Pitohui was practicing earlier *was* safe driving—to give Llenn a chance to get used to the rigors of the back seat.

Pitohui's trike was like a bullet, shooting after Summon just after he'd attacked them first.

Summon slowed down to exchange his magazine and regroup with his team, but when he saw the enemy getting rapidly larger in his side mirror, he exclaimed, "Whoa-uh!" and grabbed the handlebars with both hands, dropping down two gears with his left hand and gunning the gas with his right.

His trike began to accelerate to the best of its ability. But he had noticed too late.

"There's the first one!" said Pitohui, reaching him at a speed of nearly 110 miles per hour, coming level, and then passing. They'd been only six feet away.

A police officer would surely write up a ticket—if not for the speeding, then for the ruthless hail of bullets that Llenn poured into him. It was like spraying him with water from a hose.

Of course, at such a short range, there was no way she could miss. The bullets pelted Summon's sturdy upper half, dyeing it red with the light of lethal damage.

Above Summon's head, which was splashed with color as though a bucket of paint had been dumped over it, the DEAD tag shone. His trike slowly decelerated.

"Okay! Nice kill! Reload for the next one!"

Pitohui slowed down on the accelerator and evened out their speed. *Slower*, in this case, meant only seventy-five miles per hour. She looked behind them to check on the enemy location. This was extremely reckless when driving, the kind of stunt one could only do in the free and open safety of a vast airport tarmac.

Llenn dumped the magazine that still had a good ten shots left and dropped it over the side, then pulled a new one out of her pouch and slammed it into the P90. Including the bullet still in the chamber, that gave her fifty-one shots to use.

As soon as Llenn was done reloading, Pitohui rapidly slowed the vehicle. It decelerated from seventy-five miles per hour to under forty before spinning into a rapid U-turn.

The fact that these were all right turns was the saving grace for Llenn, who had to hold on with her left hand. If it was a left turn, she'd easily be thrown off.

Although the g-force was powerful, Llenn's will to fight was more than equal to the task.

"Next!"

But MMTM was just as motivated to fight. Two of their team were dead, and one was very injured, but they weren't going to back down now.

"Jake! Stop and take a position!"

"Roger!"

Plans were meant to change on the fly according to the circumstances. Instead of riding with the machine gun, which would be very difficult to shoot at the same time, he was going to stop and set it up—resting atop the trike.

That left David and Bold as mobile fighters. They would gang up on one trike together and try to guide it into Jake's line of fire.

Jake stopped the trike sideways, then rested the machine gun on the seat. He was between the runway and the taxiway. David observed the patterns on the ground, memorizing the locations, and said, "Keep up, Bold!"

"Got it!"

He and the man who wore his hair in locs zoomed off toward the distant target of Pitohui.

"Hello, M? Mr. M, what are we supposed to do now?"

Fukaziroh was using M's monocular to watch Jake stop his trike and set up the machine gun.

They were quite a long distance away from where the main fighting was happening. While Pitohui and Llenn engaged in combat, this trike had distanced itself entirely.

M stopped the vehicle more than four-fifths of a mile away from Jake. "We wait here for now. When Pito is racing around and attacking and raising hell, we'd only be getting in the way."

"Makes sense."

Pitohui's idea was to zoom and screech around and have Llenn do all the shooting, so they couldn't just barge in and interfere. Sowing chaos with the grenade launchers wasn't an option, either.

"Don't you think we could at least take out that machine gunner? Both my feminine wiles and my explosives could do the trick," she suggested.

"Not nearly enough range," M said. "He'd shoot us before we got close enough."

The longest effective range of Fukaziroh's MGL-140 grenade

launchers was a quarter of a mile. It would be quite a reckless idea.

"Hmm."

But Fukaziroh did not give up. She wanted to pop out a brilliant little nugget of a plan and shower in the adulation of the rest of her team. She wanted to be the star.

"What if you go alone and sneak up with your shield, then snipe him? I can stay here and cheer for you," she offered.

"It's not the worst idea…"

"Right?"

"But I feel like the whole thing will be finished before then."

"Ohhh."

"Let's goooo!" roared Pitohui as her trike zipped across the runway.

Once again, their speed was over a hundred miles an hour. The engine squealed like never before, and the body of the vehicle shook and shuddered.

Pitohui kept herself as low as possible to reduce resistance, which meant the wind was hitting Llenn that much harder. Her hat was tilted all the way forward, still on her head only because this was a virtual world that kept it stuck there.

But despite the insane rigors, Llenn's body and eyes were getting used to the strain. And she had a very good bead on the two trikes rushing after them.

The two MMTM riders were hanging on desperately, trying to keep Pitohui from slipping away. *GGO* was supposed to be a shooter game, but in this case, it had become a racing game.

They knew exactly how far Llenn's effective range was with the P90, so they kept their distance to a solid eight hundred feet. She tried to aim at them a few times, but between the distance and the vibration of the trike, her bullet circle was completely wild. She couldn't possibly hit them like this, so she didn't waste the bullets.

For ten seconds, the three bikes continued their high-speed chase. After which, Llenn said, "It's not working! They're not coming any closer!"

"Then we'll have to come up with a different idea."

"What if we try to lure them over toward M and Fuka?" Llenn suggested. She thought it was a pretty good idea.

"They'd figure that out before it worked. More importantly…," Pitohui prompted, letting go of the left handlebar and opening her window quickly, tweaking her inventory. First, she was driving while distracted; now she was doing it one-handed with her smartphone out—in a manner of speaking.

A large plasma grenade, commonly known as a "grand grenade," appeared before her. The object, a sphere the size of a small watermelon, plonked onto the tank and nestled itself between Pitohui's thighs.

"Here, Llenn."

She reached her hand around her back to offer the object to her partner. Llenn rested the P90 on her lap and accepted the grenade in the palm of her hand. She did not have a high strength stat, so it felt heavy. There was no way she could throw it far. She used both hands to clutch it so that she didn't drop it.

Clearly, the idea was that she'd use the explosive to attack the two trikes chasing them.

"Pito, do you really think I'll hit them? If they see me drop it, they'll just drive around it and be fine."

It seemed like a desperate move to her. Llenn was constantly surprised and impressed by Pitohui's intuition and creativity in battle, but this time she couldn't help being skeptical.

"You don't have to hit them with it. Get it? You see…"

As he pursued Pitohui's three-wheeled motorcycle, determined to strike if she gave him the opportunity, David saw the pink shrimp drop something onto the asphalt. It looked like a grand grenade—it had to be that.

Bold noticed it at the same time. "Grand grenade! Dodge!

Dodge! Dodge!" he warned before David could say anything. They split to either side of it to stay away from its wide blast radius, thereby limiting their exposure to the explosion. David went right, and Bold banked left.

The grand grenade rolled and rolled and continued right on past them.

"Huh?" "Huh?"

Pitohui's trike reversed and backed right after it, chasing the bomb. As a matter of fact, both the explosive and the trike were still moving *forward*, but David and Bold were going so much faster that it looked like they were rolling backward.

The uniform color and lack of features of the asphalt, and the fact that the pink shrimp was sitting in reverse position, made the illusion all the more convincing.

The grand grenade continued to pull away from them, remaining intact. Pitohui's trike went with it, after her sharp brake.

The activator on the grenade had never been pressed.

"Shit!"

By the time they realized it had been a trick, it was already too late.

Pitohui gunned the accelerator again, racing after Bold, who had shot far past her on the left. She caught up to him in moments, pulled level, and then passed him.

"Get him!" she yelled.

"On it!"

Llenn fired the P90, held sideways in her right hand, on full auto.

Because the gun was horizontal, the recoil that normally pushed upward moved it side to side as it fired. Bold tried to lift his Beretta ARX160 assault rifle to shoot back, but he was too late.

Since she was shooting one-handed, the bullets sprayed, but the P90's fifteen-shots-a-second frequency was deadly. The liberal flow of 5.7 mm rounds spread out in a horizontal array. Three of them struck Bold's forehead.

The speed at which his hit points dropped made it clear that it was an insta-kill.

"Damn youuuu! Not again, you pink pip-squeaaak!" cursed Bold as he died. His hand was fixed in place, meaning the trike continued to drive off, carrying a corpse.

It would probably continue all the way to the northern edge of the map.

"Got him!" Llenn cheered.

Pitohui shouted, "Hold on with your left hand!"

She braked hard and went into a left turn. Promptly, the vicinity was full of stabbing bullet lines.

"Eep!" Llenn instinctively ducked, looking for the source of the lines.

It was David.

"Huh?"

Neither of his hands were on the handlebars of the trike. In fact, he was standing up in the saddle, holding his assault rifle firmly with both hands. And the vehicle continued to ride at a steady speed.

"Howww?"

David began his assault like an archer on horseback—only with hot lead instead of arrows. Bullets roared all around Llenn as they traced the paths of the bullet lines.

"Hyaaa!"

The bullets whizzed past her ears. *Don't hit me, don't hit me, don't hit me!* Llenn repeated, like some kind of magic spell.

Then she heard Pitohui grunt, "Hrrg!"

"Ah!" Llenn looked at her party member's hit point bar in the upper left and saw that Pitohui's was shrinking quickly.

"I'm all right," she reassured, her HP stopping at 80 percent. "He only hit me on the side of my boob. The perv!"

"That's good," said Llenn, relieved, when there was an explosion on the left of the trike without warning.

"Urgh!" "Gaaaah!"

It blew the front left tire upward and clean off, jolting Pitohui and Llenn to the side. The trike had been in the midst of a left turn, so the blast and horizontal g-force threw them hard to the right.

"Pito! We're gonna tip over!"

"We're fine! Raaah!"

Pitohui jolted the handlebars to the right. Right wheel screaming, the trike shifted from a left turn into a right. That forced the weight into the opposite direction, redirecting the momentum to prevent it from rolling over.

The trike rode on for a few moments on just its right and rear wheels, until its body steadily evened out. Then Pitohui warned, "Hold on tight, Llenn!"

"Hu—eep?!"

The body of the trike came down onto the ground where the left wheel was missing.

Although Pitohui was braking, they were still going over fifty miles per hour. It scraped against the asphalt, tearing parts off and creating a shower of sparks as more and more of the trike broke away.

"Yeep! Ouch!"

A number of them struck Llenn's right side as they came off, because she was sitting on the rear seat facing backward.

The trike gradually slowed down, creating a constant stream of sparks all the while. It was Pitohui's sheer tenacity that kept them from tipping over. Despite missing its left front wheel and several parts below, the trike was able to slow down intact until it came to a stop on the side of the runway.

"Ahhh…"

The moment it stopped, Llenn tumbled weakly off the back seat and plopped onto the asphalt on the left side of the vehicle.

Pitohui was still straddling the trike, grinning. "You've done it now, Daveed! M, my precious wheels are ruined. You have to pay off the rest of the loan."

M replied, "Wait there. We'll come to rescue you."

"Don't come here! Daveed's riding around with his gun in both hands, shooting the rifle and grenades both. He'll attack you if you get any closer."

"Hmm? How's he doing that?"

"Dunno. Maybe he picked up a new acrobatic trick or two?"

"Nice!"

From a distance, David confirmed that Pitohui's trike had stopped. Since he wasn't controlling his handlebars, his own vehicle was simply driving straight ahead, taking him farther and farther from Pitohui.

He released his right hand from the rifle and reached toward the accelerator grip—and removed the combat knife he'd stuck into it to keep it fixed in place. David put the knife back into the sheath over his chest and grabbed the handlebar directly.

The hard rubber accelerator handle had a hole it in from the knife's point and would probably split and fall off if he stabbed it again. Or perhaps it would be designated DAMAGED, vanishing into a spray of polygonal shards.

The accelerator gambit was something he'd come up with on the spot, but it would probably only be possible one more time.

"Jake! I knocked the poisonous bird out of the sky! Can you aim at her?"

"She's about a thousand yards off! It's a bit far, but I can keep her in check!"

"Good, do it! Don't let them get away until I can arrive!"

"Okay!"

Jake prepared to blast in full auto at Pitohui and Llenn now that they were stationary. As he had warned, they were quite far away, too far for anyone to seriously consider aiming at them. And the wind was stronger than a few moments before, providing the occasional gust that would throw shots off farther.

But a 7.62 mm bullet was plenty heavy enough to carry that far, and it still packed a punch. Jake peered through the scope of the HK21 set up on his trike seat. In the distance, Pitohui and

Llenn were the size of tiny beans. He aimed higher to account for the projectile falling over distance. He timed his pulse so that the bullet circle was as small as possible and centered over the two.

Then, hoping to keep them occupied and maybe even co-incidentally strike them, he taunted, "Here's a present!" and unleashed a number of ten-shot bursts.

Pitohui detected the bullet lines, and rather than warn Llenn verbally, promptly grabbed her tiny partner by the neck with one hand and hurled her over to the right side of the trike.

"Gyaaa! Pito, what was that for?"

Then Pitohui herself leaped nimbly over the side of the vehicle as machine-gun fire struck all around them, bouncing off the ground and kicking up asphalt.

"Hya!"

It sounded like there were firecrackers going off in every direction. The gun itself was shooting from so far away that they could barely hear it.

Gagank! That loud clang was a sign that a bullet had struck the left side of the trike. It couldn't run anymore, so it didn't matter, but Llenn was worried about the possibility it might explode.

Vehicles in *GGO* had a predisposition to exploding spectacularly. When a bullet was determined to have struck and ruptured the gas tank, they would blow into smithereens in an orange explosion.

If you shot a car in real life, it'd only make a hole. There wouldn't be any fire. At least, not that easily. The conditions would have to be terrible to explode the entire car, like if the gasoline evaporated inside the cabin and ignited.

But this was the world of *GGO*. Vehicles were designed to explode quite easily from gunshots, once you got past certain armor types. Otherwise, having a vehicle would be an overwhelming advantage and destroy the competitive balance.

A truck's fuel tank was on the bottom of the body, so they didn't get hit by bullets very easily, but on a motorcycle or a trike like these, it was found on the upper part of the body.

While riding, the bullets would hit the riders first, so Llenn wasn't as worried about the secondary damage, but now the situation was different. The idea that the trike that had zipped around with them on top might become a bomb that could engulf them in an explosion in an instant was a terrifying thought.

As she lay on the ground behind it, Llenn turned to her teammate and asked, "Pito, is this bad? We might blow up!"

"Yes! It's very bad! And not like 'bad as in good'! I mean bad-bad!"

"You sound like you're having fun, though…"

Llenn craned her neck upward to look around. She saw that the bullet lines in the air above them were not actually that dense. And since she could hardly hear the shots, that meant the shooting was coming from far away. The aim was vague, then. She could probably get away by sprinting.

"Pito, let's run for it! It's better than staying here!"

"That's true, but I can't really do that. I'm on a diet," said Pitohui, and she lifted her left foot so Llenn could see it.

"Ugh!"

That was when Llenn learned that Pitohui's slim left leg was missing from the knee downward. The side where it was severed was as clean and straight as broken glass, and glowing green with a wire-frame outline.

"It was the grenade. But I'm lucky it only did this much!"

"…"

Llenn quickly glanced to the upper left. Pitohui's hit points were lower now, around 60 percent. She hadn't noticed the shift at all.

She looked back to Pitohui and saw that her leg wasn't the only part that was damaged. Red damage effects were glowing on her arm, chest, and side, all over her left half.

That was from the shrapnel of the grenade. But considering where the trike's tire had blown up, Llenn came to another realization.

Pitohui had seen the bullet circle for David's grenade and

leaned herself to the left to protect Llenn from the shrapnel. It was the only explanation for all the damage she suffered—and for Llenn's perfect health.

"Pito..."

"Yes, yes, it's not over."

Pitohui injected herself with the emergency med kit. Her entire body glowed briefly, initiating the turtle's-pace healing effect that would give her back 30 percent of her health over three whole minutes.

Loss of fingers or limbs took two minutes to automatically regrow in *GGO*, but until then, Pitohui couldn't run. And with Llenn's low strength stat, there was no way she could carry her friend. Instead, she would need to rely on her teammates.

"M! Fuka! We're trapped by a machine gun and a trike! Pito lost a leg and can't run! Do something!"

Fukaziroh responded, "Well, whining to us won't get you far... What say you, M?"

"It's a grim situation."

"Awww...," whined Llenn. She decided she should try to think of something on her own and suggested, "I could run and try to fight MMTM's leader one-on-one..."

"And you'd get shot and killed before you get him in the effective range of the P90. He's good at shooting grenades to keep you at bay, then picking you off with his rifle. You can't match him now that he's got both hands to use. Even your speed can't overcome him now," came Pitohui's quick and accurate assessment.

"Awww... In that case..."

But she was out of ideas now—except for one.

"Then as a last resort, you should run away on your own, Llenn. Meet up with M, get away from here, and focus on survival. There's no need for three unharmed people to expose themselves to danger on account of one injured member."

"What about you, Pito?"

"Daveed's obviously coming after me out of personal enmity,

so I'll try to hang in the fight here until my leg grows back," said Pitohui, lifting her beloved KTR-09 with its drum magazine.

She pulled the lever back a bit to check if it was loaded. Sometimes violent action caused a magazine to get dislodged, or the loading lever got pulled without a bullet inside, so it was important to check it often.

As she did this, machine-gun fire pelted the area ceaselessly, occasionally striking the trike.

"Go! Get a move on! You're going to fight Boss, aren't you? Didn't you make a woman's promise? Listen, you're only putting yourself underfoot hanging around here!"

"Ugh… Well, Pito…good luck!" Llenn said at last, glancing back at the bullet lines before leaping out from cover.

She went the opposite direction from where David was. It put her closer to the enemy machine gun, but she knew she could avoid the lines from this distance.

After a bit of zigzagging, she finally wondered, *Wait, which way am I supposed to be going?*

"Llenn! Can you point yourself west-northwest? That's where you'll find us!"

"Thanks! But what about Pito?"

Jake seemed to have noticed Llenn and was sending more shots her way. That was a good thing, because it meant less danger to Pitohui.

Watching carefully for bullet lines, Llenn kicked it up to top gear. Every last projectile hit asphalt helplessly behind her.

"Pito is… Well, Pito is Pito, so she'll manage! Don't worry!" said Fukaziroh worryingly.

"Sorry, Leader! The pink shrimp got away!" said Jake.

"That means it's only Pitohui behind that trike!" said David. His mind was made up. He'd been running the trike slowly and watching out for M, but now he pointed it toward Pitohui.

"Keep her down, but watch out for the other trike! We're going to take her down for good!"

"Roger that!"

Jake pulled the trigger of the machine gun, and David tugged the accelerator of the trike. MMTM began to zero in on Pitohui alone.

As David's trike started small and distant and rapidly grew larger, Pitohui muttered, "Yeah, that's not good. M, you take it from here." It was practically her last will.

No, Pito! Don't give up! Llenn thought but did not say.

Pitohui had essentially accepted her own death to allow Llenn to escape. That was the one thing she couldn't tell her teammate in return.

Instead, she sprinted at maximum speed, her back turned, and prayed. *I don't care what miracle or coincidence it has to be, or what god or devil or spirit of death—just send your gust of heavenly wind to protect Pito.*

At that very moment, the breeze went still and silent.

As he reached a distance of six hundred yards from his hated rival, David held on to the Steyr STM-556 hanging from a sling around his neck with just his left arm. His hand was around the magazine so that he could fire a grenade, rather than bullets.

"Keep up the covering fire! I'm going in!"

"Roger that!"

David had tasted defeat twice in Squad Jam thanks to Pitohui. He revved the trike. He could see the path to victory.

David would drive toward Pitohui doing high-speed slaloms, avoiding her bullet lines if necessary. He was going to close in to where she sat all alone in the middle of nothing. Of course, he would avoid coming from the opposite direction as Jake so that he didn't get hit by a stray shot. A forty-five-degree angle would be best.

Once he was within four hundred yards, he would stick the knife into the accelerator grip and switch to two-handed aim again. Then he would shoot her with all the grenades he could—if he scored a direct hit, great. If he missed, he could shoot her with the rifle while she was taken aback.

Conveniently for him, the gusty wind chose this moment to calm down. That would make aiming with the grenade launcher easier.

"*This* time!" snarled David, baring his canines in triumph.

Then Jake exploded and died.

Or to be more accurate, the trike he was stationed behind exploded.

It was one of those classic *GGO* vehicular explosions, and before Jake could even react, he was blasted into polygonal pieces by flame and explosive force.

When he saw the orange light of the explosion, David slowed the accelerator and gasped, "What...the...?!"

A few seconds later, the sound of the explosion reached his ears.

"Whut? The bad guy blew up? What happened?"

Fukaziroh, too, saw the distant explosion.

"I don't know, but the situation's changed. Let's go!" said M, who checked through the scope of the M14 EBR, then swung the weapon over his back and started to drive the trike again.

"Pito!" he shouted. "Enemy machine gun is silent! The reverse side is safe! We're heading there now! Hang in there!"

"Oh? I don't know what that's all about, but...sure thing."

Pitohui hopped up onto her one foot, then bounced over to the other side of the trike to hide where the bullets had been flying at her before.

Once she was there, she murmured, "So what god saved me?"

"Amazing! Was that your shot, M? Or was it you, Fuka?" marveled Llenn, who stopped running and turned around to look at the black smoke rising in the distance.

"Neither of us," said Fukaziroh. "It wasn't you?"

"How would I do that?"

"Maybe you awoke to your magical powers."

"I don't know how."

Then the both of them together wondered, "No, really, who was it?"

Behind Jake—at least, behind him when he'd been alive—inside the airport control tower that loomed over the entire vast runway area, lurked two players.

The tower had to be very tall so air traffic controllers could give instructions for takeoff and landing.

It was about three hundred feet above the ground. In the control station, which was like an observation deck walled in with glass all around, lying atop the filthy carpet, was a green-haired young woman: Shirley.

"Phew..."

She pulled the bolt handle of the R93 Tactical 2 rifle and expelled an empty cartridge. Then she pushed the handle forward again to load the next shot.

Thanks to the bullet going through it, the glass was significantly broken, the wind howling low and deep now that it was picking up again. On the other side was the vast expanse of runway asphalt.

"Nice shot! Twelve hundred yards! That's a record, a huge new record! I can vouch; I was your witness!" clamored Clarence, who was also lying on the carpet off to the left.

She was looking not through her own binoculars but through a larger pair she'd found in the room, a proper air traffic controller's binoculars.

"Shut up. I can hear you through the comm—you don't need to shout."

"You said there was no way you could hit at this distance! And you did it in one shot! Are you some kind of whiz kid, Shirley? You should change your name to *Jesus*!"

Shirley got to her feet without much hurry and glanced at Clarence's brainless smile. "I think the word you're looking for is *genius*."

"Oops! But even still, that shot was divine!" Clarence raved.

Shirley kept her tone low and explained, "I hit the vehicle. That's a bigger target than a human. Thanks to the explosive round, it blew up. And the wind quieted down for a moment, which helped. All of that was coincidental. I got lucky."

"Coincidence and luck are a part of skill! Bravo! Or are you supposed to say 'Brava!' if it's a woman? Anyway, why'd ya save Pitohui? If you let them keep going, they would have killed her for sure. You could have smiled and watched it happen from a safe place. So why?" Clarence asked, smiling.

Shirley smirked back at her and said, "Don't ask what you already know the answer to. I'm her Grim Reaper."

"……"

For several seconds, David sat on the trike in complete shock.

In the upper left of his view, Jake's hit point bar was empty, with a big *X* next to it. He had no idea why Jake's trike had blown up.

All he knew was one thing: He'd lost his chance to finish off Pitohui for good.

"Fine, then! We'll go down together in a blaze of glory!" he snarled, brows furrowed. He squeezed with his right hand, ready to drive the trike straight into her.

"Leader!"

"Ah!"

He relaxed his grip. It was the voice of his only surviving teammate, Kenta, that brought him back to his senses.

"Leader, don't die for nothing! Squad Jam is all kinds of chaos this time! We don't know what the alliance is up to! Even just the two of us, we've still got a chance to win it!"

"You're right… I got it… I'm sorry," David said. He grinned to himself, then told his teammate, "I'll go pick you up! Wait right there!"

Pitohui watched the trike speed off, lowered the KTR-09, and murmured, "Oh-ho-ho? Am I saved?"

The wind gusted again, brushing her long ponytail.

CHAPTER 11

Save This Battle for Me

SECT.11

CHAPTER 11
Save This Battle for Me

It was 1:27.

"Pitooo!"

Llenn rushed to Pitohui's side.

"Yeah! C'mon!" said Pitohui, holding out her arms in a seated position, ready for a warm embrace.

"Uh-oh!" Llenn came to a stop before she entered the hug.

"Tsk!" Pitohui sulked. Her foot was regenerating now with a shining light. Her bodysuit, boot, and the thin dagger stuck to the outside of her boot all came back.

She hopped up to her feet and said, "All right, let's run!"

"Yeah!"

They started heading to the northwest, in the direction of M and Fukaziroh. Not long after they started, a thought occurred to Llenn.

"That explosion that took out the enemy...," she said. "What was it? He didn't actually shoot his own vehicle somehow, did he?"

In *GGO*, as in real life, it was quite easy to duck down behind cover, then pop your head back up and accidentally shoot the thing you were hiding behind. The sights were on the top of the gun, so you could easily think you were aiming over it, but not have the muzzle fully clearing the obstacle.

Llenn couldn't imagine any other likely answer, but Pitohui

didn't hasten to a conclusion. "That might be it, but I don't know the truth. I suppose we can check out the footage after this is all done and compare our theories to the real answer."

"That's true. Well, at least we're still alive! That's great!"

"Just don't forget, MMTM still has two survivors out there."

"Gotcha!"

As they ran, M drove the trike back toward them. He swung around them, watching out for enemies on the horizon, then ran parallel.

"Hey, ladies! Want a ride? Forget that, there's no space for you! Just keep running, just keep running!" Fukaziroh catcalled.

M eased up on the acceleration and eventually came to a complete stop. He got off first, and then Fukaziroh jumped off the seat.

"Pito, take over driving. I'll ride on the back seat."

"Wait, what? Llenn can run on her own, but what about me?" Fukaziroh protested.

"I'll make you a seat now," said M, turning the trike's key.

The body of the trike between the two front wheels popped open a small lid. M pushed it forward, exposing a front trunk that was about big enough to hold a helmet.

"Ooh! There's a hidden chamber there! This property's looking like more and more of a deal!" Fukaziroh exclaimed.

Meanwhile, M placed significant pressure on the lid, until it went *crack!* and broke right off the hinges. He tossed the loose lid aside.

When she saw the space that it left there, Fukaziroh mumbled, "I bet you could fit three Llenns in there."

"No, you couldn't! I'm not *that* small!"

"Oh. Yeah, I guess you're right."

"But maybe two…"

"Hang on."

✳   ✳   ✳

One trike and one very small human in pink ran along the blacktop.

"Hya-haaa! Faster, Llenn, faster!"

"This is as fast as I can go!"

"No, you can do better! Are you going for the gold medal or not?! Have you forgotten the oath we made that fateful summer's day?!"

"I have no idea what you're talking about!"

The trike was currently a triple-seater, in wild violation of road safety laws.

Sitting in the front—with her butt jammed into the front trunk—was Fukaziroh. Sitting in the driver's seat and happily piloting was Pitohui. And in the back was M, with his huge back-pack jutting out over empty space.

The trike's speedometer gave a readout of 28 for miles per hour.

So it was impressive that Llenn was keeping pace with them. Her legs were speeding so fast that they were a blur; you couldn't see them clearly.

Somehow, LPFM survived their battle with MMTM. Their next destination was the northwest corner of the airport. Now that they had only one trike, combat in a wide-open zone posed greater challenges. As a result, M suggested they cross the airport with haste and get into the ruined city in the northwest part of the map. The ruins would be better for fighting up close or at midrange. And that was the best possible environment for their current team makeup.

After lots of running and lots of fighting, the vast expanse of the airport was coming to an end. They had maybe half a mile to go to the edge. Llenn started to see the chain-link fence along the highway up ahead.

Bzzt, bzzt, bzzt.

The wristwatch on Llenn's left hand vibrated. It was set to go off thirty seconds before each scan, meaning it was now 1:29:30.

From the rear seat, M craned his neck to look behind them and said, "Scan's coming up. Pito, point us away from the west and stop the trike. Llenn, hide behind it. Fuka, hop off quickly and keep an eye on the surroundings."

"Okeydoke."

"Roger that!"

"You got it."

Pitohui slowed the vehicle. They were turning their back to the west because that meant M's backpack covered the largest part of their profile from potential snipers on the highway. But if a bullet hit his head? Well, that'd be the end of that.

Before she turned the handlebars all the way, Pitohui noticed something. "Hmm? Wait, M, what about that? The hole up there on the left."

M glanced over and saw a large hole in the runway about a quarter of a mile ahead on the left. It was a huge black hole about a hundred feet across. There were chunks of material all around it, giving the flat artificial runway a little touch of natural chaos.

"That works."

"Okay, then," said Pitohui, steering the trike that way.

"Wait for me!" yelped Llenn, trying to keep up.

By the time she caught up with them, the three were already off the trike and hiding in the hole.

If they were in there, then traps weren't an issue, she decided and slid in feetfirst. Only when she went over the edge did she find out that it was actually quite a deep hole, and she was going to land in the deepest part.

"Oof!"

It was shaped like a gentle mortar, more than ten feet deep at the center. Beneath the thick asphalt was hard, dark earth. It was the perfect bunker for them to hide inside.

As she got up, Llenn asked, "What is this hole from?"

"Dunno. This is supposed to be America. Maybe Paul Bunyan caused it by pulling out weeds."

"Fuka, you have detailed knowledge of the most random things," said Pitohui. The subject of Paul Bunyan, the legendary figure from North American folklore, was not something most Japanese people knew about.

Though no one here was aware of how this hole came to be, it had actually been created about an hour earlier, when SHINC's booby trap blew up the airstairs truck.

It turned 1:30.

The third full refill of ammo happened, and the ninth Satellite Scan began.

The scan approached the map from the south.

"I wonder…if Boss's group…is still in the alliance…"

Contrary to the sinking feeling in Llenn's heart, the scan rose upward rapidly over the map.

The first ones she spotted were ZEMAL. They were set up in the crater area. It was as if they lived there.

Atop the frozen lake was the alliance. There were…six dots.

"Huh?"

Llenn tapped the blips over and over but didn't find the name SHINC.

In the southeast part of the airport were the two remaining members of MMTM. That made it clear they weren't coming back on the trike to pursue them, to Llenn's relief.

Eventually, the scan swept up to their own location. It indicated that LPFM was in the northwest part of the airport. And then…

"Ah!"

About two-thirds of a mile directly to the west, just inside the city ruins across the highway, was one more illuminated dot.

"……"

With trembling fingers, Llenn touched it.

"What?!"

SHINC.

She read the five letters three times. Each time, they remained unchanged. Boss and the gang were there. Close—very close.

"It's them!" she shouted. She was celebrating as if she'd spotted her own teammates.

As the scan proceeded, it showed that T-S was still alive about five miles away on the train tracks in the city, but that wasn't anything Llenn fretted over, so they could buzz off, for all she cared.

"Whoo-hoo! SHINC's so close! What's up with that?" Fukaziroh asked. But no one had an answer for her.

The next moment, there was a sharp cracking noise in the distance, and a light rose into the western sky.

As they all watched, a yellow flare rose high into the air against the clouded-over, reddish-gray sky. Then it descended on a little parachute, buffeted back and forth by the wind.

"Well, well, well. That must be the location of the sweet little Amazons," said Pitohui, smirking. She gave herself one more emergency med kit, just to get her HP back up to full.

"I suppose they're saying, 'Here we are. Come and get us,'" suggested M.

"That's right! That has to be it!" Llenn exclaimed, ready to sing, her fists trembling in excitement.

"Oh, I'm not so sure," said Fukaziroh gleefully. "They could have tied up Boss in a bag, braids and all, keeping her prisoner so she can't commit suicide or resign, and everyone in the alliance aside from the leaders is there so that we get surrounded by thirty people and killed in an instant."

It was hard to tell if she was saying that for effect or if she really was looking forward to it happening. Probably a bit of both.

"Ugh!"

Llenn let her trembling arms dangle with disappointment. It wasn't completely out of the question; in fact, it seemed fairly possible; in fact, it was getting more likely in her mind by the second.

"Then let's figure it out for sure. We'll send a scout," said M, waving his hand to call up the menu.

What he produced was a white mass about the size of an A4 book; it was two inches thick. He tossed it into the air, and four arms immediately slid free from the corners, deploying propellers that began to spin.

It was the drone he'd used during the playtest on the sixteenth—the one that would cost 110,000 yen in real money. An ultraconvenient luxury that would allow them to survey the area from the air.

Not only was it expensive, it had to be piloted manually, and its battery time was extremely short by design. This was an item that had very limited practical use. You couldn't just leave it floating up in the air all the time for your own convenience. If you could, it would destroy *GGO*'s competitive balance, so there was no use hoping for a buffed version.

After sending the drone aloft, M then equipped a pair of goggles that looked like scuba snorkeling eyewear. This was a new one.

"Ooh, VR goggles! Using VR goggles in a full-dive VR world! That's real creativity, M!" exclaimed Fukaziroh. It was hard to tell if she was praising him or insulting him. Probably a bit of both. At any rate, this would allow him to see what the flying drone was seeing as if his head were attached to it.

Pitohui took the tablet controller he'd used in the playtest, and she set it so Llenn and Fukaziroh could see the screen, too.

M had little controller grips in either hand. In response to his moving the thumb stick with his left hand, the drone issued the buzzing sound that was its namesake and rose higher into the air.

The device went horizontal, then zoomed over the highway and toward the ruins. The footage from the sky gave a very clear picture of the fallen city.

"There," he said and pushed the stick to lower its altitude. But not too far—just in case it put the drone into easy shooting range. With the other stick, he zoomed in with the camera.

What he witnessed was a grid of city streets, with dilapidated buildings either standing or fallen between them. Six women were using the bed of a toppled truck as a stand to stick out.

That, of course, was SHINC, Boss included. There were no other players visible in the area. Anna had a pair of binoculars, and she noticed the drone, pointing and gesturing toward it.

The next moment, all six sprang into motion.

Sophie and Rosa were on the sides. The two heavyset members did forward splits while holding their arms up in elegant circles over their heads.

Behind them, Anna and Tohma lifted their outer legs in a brilliant example of a ballet leg extension. They raised their Dragunov sniper rifles like batons.

In the very back center, the gorilla-statured woman with her hair in braids, Boss, lifted one leg high behind her, then raised her opposite arm in a perfect ballerina arabesque, which she held without budging an inch.

And in front of them all, the last member, Tanya, came running from the end of the truck and jumped before the other five. She did a somersault to a backflip with a twist, then rotated forward again and threw her arms out as she landed.

This impromptu bit of beautiful acrobatic posing from the menacing, battle-hardy women was met with cheers of admiration from LPFM.

"Ooh, amazing!"

"That's very impressive."

"Yes, very well done."

But the last member of the group screeched, "Ah-ha-ha-ha-ha-ha-ha-ha-ha-ha!"

"What is it, Llenn? Did you eat laughing shrooms?"

"Wah-ha-ha-ha-ha-ha! No! This is happy laughter! I'm happy!" Llenn insisted with tears in her eyes. From the hole in the asphalt, she shouted with all the breath in her lungs, "I'm going to do it!

This time, I'll go over to you, so we can fight for good! Just you wait!"

"You know they can't hear you, right?" said Fukaziroh reasonably.

M added, "Then let's go introduce ourselves," and pulled on the left controller stick. The drone zoomed closer and closer to SHINC as they posed, until it was thirty feet in the air above them.

Their smiles were quite apparent from this distance as they held their stances.

"And spin!"

M tilted the stick quickly, causing the image on the screen to rotate as the drone did a turn. He let go of the stick, and it froze again.

Then SHINC released their poses and stood naturally. Boss gave them an especially freakish smile and reached out with her right hand, which had no gun in it. She pointed her index finger at the camera on the drone, then flipped it upward, mimicking the recoil of a gun firing. *Bang!*

"Awww! Ya shot me!" said Fukaziroh.

The drone retreated and rose into the air. SHINC jumped off the truck and quickly scampered away to hide among the ruins.

Pitohui said, "I suppose the battle is on, then. If those girls were camping at a spot where they could see the highway, they'd be able to snipe us with their antitank rifle. How very sporting of them not to do such a thing."

As M flew the drone back before its battery drained all the way, he said, "Indeed. They would have had the advantage. It'd make it hard for us to even approach their location."

"They're true samurai. I trust you have no lingering regrets, Llenn?"

"None!" she said, turning to Fukaziroh with a huge smile. "I'm going out to kill them for a bit!" she announced as casually as if she were merely going to the convenience store.

"Wait a second. You're not going alone. Are we a team or not?" demanded Fukaziroh.

But M muttered, "No, that's a good tactic."

The drone returned to the hole in the ground. Soon after, the pink pip-squeak was the first to leave, followed by the three others. A man watched it all happen through his binoculars.

He wore sunglasses, a face mask, and bright-green camo gear.

And he was watching from within a ruined yellow school bus abandoned on the highway. He was hidden firmly, flat on his stomach in the rear of the bus, with a little space near a broken window and the rear door for observation and sniping. Even his camouflage was perfect, making it clear that he was an experienced player.

"LPFM are on the move. Four targets. They're crossing the highway to make contact with SHINC," he murmured into his comm.

Into his ear returned the response. "Good. We'll head there once they've crossed over."

"Roger that. I could shoot them all the moment they cross the road, though. What should I do?" the man asked. He lowered the binoculars and fingered the gun resting on a bipod next to him.

The weapon was a Heckler & Koch M110A1 automatic sniper rifle, painted in the same camo pattern as his uniform. It was a 7.62 mm caliber gun. Specifically, 7.62 × 51 mm NATO.

This armament had a particularly tricky history. It started off as a German sniper rifle known as the G26, which was built with the body of the HK417 assault rifle. The M110A1 was an improved build of the G26 that was sold to the American army and given a new name.

The Americans already had a gun called the M110 that they'd been using, but while it looked almost the same, it was from a completely different company. The presence or absence of the *A1* at the end made a huge difference in which weapon you were talking about. It could be very confusing.

In *GGO*, the M110A1 was introduced as one of the top-level automatic sniper rifles, very high quality and very expensive.

As the masked man said, if Llenn's group started to cross the highway about thirteen hundred feet away, he could easily take them out with a merciless burst of automatic shooting.

From his earpiece came the reply. "No, that's fine. Let SHINC be their opponent. That was our deal, technically. I'll have the scout keep an eye on them, too. If SHINC loses, take them out at once. And if they win—take *them* out at once."

"Got it. What if either of them spots me and attacks?" the masked man asked.

The distant man replied in a clinical manner, neither pleased nor annoyed. "If that happens, then the deal doesn't matter anymore. We'll escort both teams out of the game together."

"Got it."

Llenn crossed the highway.

She ran at the speed of which only she was capable, sidestepping and zigzagging all the way.

Her destination was the ruined city before her eyes. To the battlefield where SHINC waited.

Moments earlier, M said, "First we'll have Llenn charge in. Look for SHINC, then start fighting however you like when you find them. But don't forget: We have to stick firm to the hit-and-run strategy. Don't push too hard trying to finish the enemy on your own. And do not stop under any circumstances. Always stay on the move; always keep the battlefield in flux."

"Mm-hmm."

"We'll approach using the gunshots as a guide. In the open

streets, Fuka's grenade launchers will provide effective backup. Pitohui will be Fuka's support. I'll stay back farther and look for an ideal sniping position."

Llenn figured it out. "I got it! So it's the same as in SJ1, right?"

"That's right. SHINC works as a six-person team, which means your ability to act alone at high speed in their midst will be most, effective."

"Gotcha!" she replied with gusto.

Fukaziroh asked, "But, Mr. M, what if they see that coming and react to take advantage of it?"

"Then that's what happens. Let us pray. But I do have this strategy…"

I don't mind people praying, if that's what it takes for me to battle with the gang! Llenn sang to herself as she crossed the highway and charged toward the abandoned city.

There was only one thought on her mind.

This battle is mine!

"Llenn's charging us. Keep your eye on the surroundings, everyone!" Boss warned her team as she stared through the binoculars. Her smile was both delightful and diabolical.

SHINC was in a defensive circle within the ruins. In the center of a crossroads where hundred-foot-wide streets intersected, in fact.

Tall buildings still stood on the corners of the intersection, meaning there was no way to snipe at them or shoot grenades from a longer distance unless you climbed those buildings.

Wide roads led north, south, east, and west. By a pile of rubble stacked on the east side was Rosa, PKM machine gun at the ready. On the opposite side was her combo partner, Anna, with a Dragunov sniper rifle.

On the south side, Tohma's PTRD-41 antitank rifle was steadied against the ground in firing position. Her Dragunov was also at her side, where she could grab it to fire if needed.

Sophie was near Tohma as well, ready to pick up and carry the antitank rifle should they need to move it.

There was no rubble near them, so they had a number of gray ponchos arranged over themselves for camouflage. There was even one over the long barrel of the PTRD-41, though it would easily get shaken off if it actually fired a single shot.

Tanya was hunched on the northwest corner, alternating checks on the north and west directions, where they were least likely to see any enemies. The "secret weapon" they'd found in the ruins was waiting right next to her.

Boss waited in the center of the intersection, inside a van with popped tires, on the lookout.

Based on studying previous Squad Jams, Boss was absolutely certain of one thing: Llenn was going to come charging at them alone.

As they waited in the city, she would employ a high-speed hit-and-run tactic, and while they were occupied chasing her and otherwise being stirred up, the others would come to blast them with grenades and snipe them.

And Llenn would happily accept that role.

So Boss made a decision: She would not split up the team's strength. She would not be distracted and pushed out of her comfort zone. And that meant that if she glimpsed Llenn or if Llenn poked at them, she would not react at once.

So when Tohma caught sight of a pink blur on the street to the south through her scope and called out, "It's Llenn!" the only reply Boss made was "Don't shoot."

Once the target was out of sight, she followed that up with, "Okay, now follow her."

Llenn ran and ran at top speed.

Over three minutes had passed since she ran into the city and proceeded up and down the wide-open streets, left and right. She was sprinting, so the actual distance she covered was considerable. She even passed by the truck they saw from the drone.

In the meantime, between watching out for snipers from the windows or the inside of cars and looking for booby-trap wires in the street, Llenn's mind was as tense as possible. The mental strain of paying so much attention was tremendous.

She wanted to slow down a bit and relax, to conserve some mental energy for the actual gunfight, but that wasn't an option.

Stop, and you'll be a target. The best defense is staying in motion.

Llenn continued running.

Running was her entire strategy.

Tanya stayed in pursuit of Llenn.

After Tohma spotted Llenn, Tanya rushed after her. She saw Llenn turn at a distant intersection about three hundred yards ahead.

Llenn turned left, so Tanya rushed to that corner. She glanced around the side of the building and caught a glimpse of pink, and as soon as she saw Llenn make another turn, she rushed after that corner again.

Since Llenn was faster than her, Tanya was only keeping up with the help of the "secret weapon."

The only thing that could enable her to move faster was a vehicle. But an engine would make noise that drew attention. Being surrounded by building walls meant significantly more echo, so it wouldn't take very long to blow her cover.

Tanya's secret weapon did not make extra noise, however. It used no fuel. It had no batteries.

It did require a whole lot of pedaling, though.

"Raaaaah!"

Tanya's vehicle was a bicycle. In the ruins, she'd found a single rusty mountain bike that was still rideable, and she'd brought it with her.

As Risa Kusunoki in real life, a girl with excellent athletic ability, Tanya's high agility allowed her to ride faster than Llenn could run, provided she pedaled as hard as she could. She could afford to wait for Llenn to turn a corner and still catch up in time.

Even when Tanya had a clear view of Llenn's back before turning, she did not take any shots.

A big part of that was the fact that the 9 mm Parabellum bullets her Bizon fired were not meant for this kind of distance. But mainly, it was because her purpose was to follow Llenn, not attack.

Tanya's duty was to figure out where Llenn was going and estimate when she would appear near the squad's location. She was very frustrated about how she was Llenn's first victim in SJ1, but she sacrificed her own ambition for the sake of the team.

It was true that when a character with very high agility raced across the map at high speed, there was a direction where caution fell to the wayside.

That direction was the rear. When you were fast enough, you didn't care as much about the rear. There was so much visual information to the front and sides that it took all of your concentration to parse everything.

Boss had ordered Tanya to follow her because she had a hunch that Llenn wasn't going to look back the direction she'd come, or turn around on her heels and reverse directions. That hunch was correct; for over a minute, Llenn had failed to notice Tanya following her. The high-speed runner with a trailing bicyclist stayed in formation without fail. They turned here and there in unerring unison, like a pen tracing a path through a maze on paper.

Then, at last, Tanya got the chance she was waiting for.

Llenn turned left at a corner and saw a building had fallen and blocked the road, leaving a right turn as her only option. In the intersection beyond that, she would run into the rest of SHINC, having just shifted positions enough to avoid a monster swarm.

This was one of the "trap points" they'd chosen ahead of time. The buildings around the corner were on the shorter side. Though the ruined city was like a maze, Tanya had great confidence in her mental map. In the several minutes between their ride in the masked team's Humvee and the Satellite Scan, she had plenty of time to ride around on the bike and memorize the map.

As the pursuing wolf, Tanya never slowed down on the pedals. Through the comm, she warned her team, "Rabbit's entering the net from the north. I repeat, the rabbit has entered the net from the north."

Boss replied, "Roger. Rosa, Anna, and Tohma, point your claws accordingly. I'll watch the rear and sky."

That meant the three of them would have their guns facing north, set up with ponchos or in special hiding positions that would keep them out of view.

Please, please, be in time, Tanya prayed.

Then Boss gave her the good news. "Positions have been changed. The net is cast. I don't see any drones overhead."

If they were being watched from above, the whole thing would be ruined, so they were very cautious of M's drone. So far, it hadn't made a second appearance.

"Yes! I'll watch the exit!"

Tanya hopped off the bike and grabbed her Bizon. With a quick swipe of the menu, she put the sling back in her inventory so that it didn't catch on anything while firing.

Next, she pressed the stock against her shoulder to steady it for shooting at any moment, then began to run on her own two feet this time.

If Llenn turned back to escape in this direction, Tanya would gun down her prey without mercy.

"Who would you bet on? SHINC or Llenn?"

"SHINC."

"Me too."

"Amazons, of course."

"At this point, poor Llenn doesn't stand a chance."

The odds were extremely low for SHINC in the bar, meaning everyone expected them to win. If you bet on Llenn here, and she won, the payout would be a jackpot.

On the screen, she was still running. There was a silencer on her P90's muzzle, presumably for urban battle. The gun was in both hands in front of her body, and she ran like an arrow shot from a bow.

Thanks to the collapsed building ahead, she would eventually be unable to turn left or continue straight. When she was forced to turn right, to the south, SHINC would be lying in wait just two hundred yards ahead at the next intersection.

The road was straight. Crumbling, dilapidated buildings about five stories tall lined the street, but they had no open doors or windows to run inside for shelter.

If Llenn came down the street, she would be facing SHINC and take fire from machine guns, sniper rifles, and an antitank rifle. No matter how fast Llenn was, she couldn't escape all of that at once.

"It would be one thing if all of LPFM was there, but Llenn alone is asking for trouble."

"Exactly. Why would she use such a desperate strategy?"

"Maybe she's okay with losing, as long as it's to SHINC?"

"I didn't think she was the type to do that…"

"It's too reckless. M's gotten sloppy, I think."

But while the viewers' opinions were given freely and without consequence, Llenn continued on her way.

"Good luck, li'l pinky!"

"Don't give up!"

One group was aggressively in her corner. Nobody in the pub realized it was actually Team DOOM.

On the screen, Llenn ran and ran. The corner was just 150 yards away.

Once she leaped around it, she'd meet a hail of gunfire from SHINC. There would be no escape.

Seventy yards.

The pub was silent now.

Ready to watch the little pink pip-squeak, who had won SJ1, come in second in SJ2, and won SJ3, get shot full of holes.

Thirty yards.

"Good-bye, Llenn."

Ten yards...

She jumped.

On the screen, three things happened at the same time.

Llenn leaped out into the street.

SHINC saw her and opened fire.

And—in the midpoint between them, directly in the center of the street, a plasma grenade exploded.

The pale-blue discharge created a sphere that gouged out the ground, shook the air, and deflected upward all the bullets shot at it.

That included Rosa's PKM, Anna's Dragunov, and Tohma's PTRD-41.

Protected behind its shield, Llenn spoke to the rest of her team.

"Thanks, Fuka! SHINC's in the center of the intersection!"

"No thanks needed! Let's get 'em!"

"Everyone, run! Grenades incoming!" Boss screamed. Each member of SHINC got up as quickly as she could and retreated toward the entrance of a ruined building.

The building had previously been a multiuse mall of some kind, and the first floor was wide open, with broken windows that made it possible to leap inside from just about anywhere.

After the five of them vanished, bullet lines arced down into the center of the intersection from the southeast, with two plasma grenades erasing them and landing in succession. They blew everything in the intersection to bits, like an act of very aggressive cleaning.

A blast of wind carried dust through the entrance to the building, rattling SHINC.

"Gaaah! Why?!" Boss gasped, taken aback. "The drone wasn't flying around. How did they know we were here?"

"Huh? What? An attack?"

"It's the grenadier girl... How did they know SHINC's location?"

The men who'd expected to see Llenn die had their jaws slack in shock. Nobody recognized how LPFM had known.

I can't believe that really worked! Llenn thought, her heart leaping, and she plunged through the cloud of dust caused by the explosions.

Fukaziroh wasn't going to be shooting any more grenades, so Llenn bolted straight through without mercy. There was just one thing for her to do: use the dust clouds as cover to zip around to wherever SHINC was in the vicinity of the intersection, and shoot them dead with her P90—or die trying.

The strategy was as follows.

The idea that M came up with before sending Llenn out on her mad dash was a truly bizarre one.

He expanded the map's zooming function over the city ruins, right to the place where was Llenn was running now. Then he pointed at a spot on the wrecks and told her to go in here, then run around all over at top speed and narrate her directions over the comm as she went.

For example...

"I turned right at the first corner.

"Left after that.

"Went left at the second intersection."

And so on.

Llenn was skeptical. She could do it, but why?

M replied, "Based on your actions, I'll surmise SHINC's ambush location. To maximize mobility, I bet they'll be hiding out at an intersection rather than inside buildings. And they aren't going to shoot until they're certain they have a sure kill. The more you travel, the more I can narrow it down by saying, 'You didn't get shot here and here, so therefore, it's likely they're over *here*.' Once I can tell where they're lying in wait, I'll have Fuka shoot a plasma grenade to block their bullets, right as you're about to come into view."

Llenn decided to go along with the plan. It was the kind of thing that would be impossible if you didn't have full trust in Fukaziroh's ability to shoot her grenade launchers exactly where she aimed.

And it was *also* the kind of thing that would be impossible if you didn't have full trust in M's stalkerish ability to move around naturally while predicting his target's future location.

Do it! Do it! Do it!

Llenn raced through the dust clouds, psyching herself up for the moment, when—*bshk!*

"Ouch!"

She was shot through the left shoulder from behind. As she didn't have much toughness when it came to getting attacked, that cost a tenth of her health.

For an instant, she was torn between charging ahead and dropping to the ground, and then the choice was made for her when she tripped over a rock and fell.

"Blrbf!"

As the dust from the first explosion slowly cleared, bright-red bullet lines extended over her head like searchlights. Bullets came whipping through the air, following the lines. She did not hear any gunshots.

It's Tanya! She was behind me! Following me!

A shiver ran up Llenn's back. She now realized she'd been so confident charging forward that it had nearly cost her life.

Tanya had been firing at full auto at a target she couldn't see, which meant the bullet that hit her was just a lucky shot. But Llenn's luck was that it was only the shoulder.

Continuing to charge forward while Tanya had an open shot from behind wasn't an option. Llenn thanked the rock that had tripped her.

"Tanya's behind me! I'll turn back and get her first! You guys get Boss and the rest!"

"Got it! Good luck!" said Fukaziroh in her ear as Llenn turned back in the direction she believed the bullet lines had come from and fired the P90.

"Llenn's coming this way!"

The corner of the building behind which Tanya was hiding chipped and scraped away as bullets gouged its surface. She could hardly hear the gunshots behind the sound of the contact, so it was definitely Llenn's P90.

"Okay, she's all yours!" said Boss.

Tanya nimbly hopped back several times. Llenn didn't want to get shot in the back, so she'd surely come for her first. Now it was Tanya's role to pull back as far as possible, to lead Llenn away from the rest of the team.

A whirlwind that billowed up between the buildings blew the dust clouds away.

Tanya and Llenn exchanged their magazines at the same time.

A fifty-three-round 9 mm Parabellum helical-feed cylinder magazine and a fifty-round 5.7 mm stick magazine fit inside the Bizon and P90, respectively.

Through the dissipating dust, Llenn clearly saw the outline of the building's corner. Around the corner to the left, from her perspective, she should find Tanya—lying in wait for her.

Llenn barely held back her urge to jump around the corner and fire wildly. Instead, she stopped ten feet away, kept her gun aimed at the space in front of it, and called out, "Hey, how are you? I'm glad we're finally getting to fight!"

"So am I! On behalf of my squad, I'm very thankful!" came Tanya's voice around the corner.

Llenn couldn't see her, but she could tell that Tanya was waiting with her gun out, like her, at about the same spot on the other side of the corner.

She didn't launch herself around the edge. This was only the first opponent from SHINC. She wasn't looking for a mutual death here.

Instead, Llenn quietly called to her trusty friends for assistance.

"Eighty yards north, twenty yards west from initial shot. Calling in one plasma. Over and out."

Fukaziroh heeded Llenn's order by adjusting the aim of her MGL-140. She was sitting on the roof of a ten-story multiuse building about three hundred yards away, with the grenade launcher propped between her legs, splayed out in front of her. It was Fukaziroh's own inimitable style of bombardment.

She couldn't see the spot she'd struck just moments ago, but the pillar of smoke was visible, so she knew exactly where she was firing. All she had to do was adjust accordingly.

Pomp!

With a cute, hollow sound, a single, blue-tipped grenade flew out.

"It's awaaay!"

Llenn heard her call out, "Hiiit!"

"Now!"

With exact timing and unerring accuracy, the plasma grenade landed on target and literally obliterated everything within a thirty-foot radius.

Its target was the top of the building where Llenn and Tanya were facing off. The building was already falling apart, and this was certainly going to finish it off.

A huge hole was opened on the roof of the five-story building, and the shock of the blast left it unable to stand on its own; the structure crumbled inward. A tremendous, earth-shaking rumbling ensued.

"Nice shot! Thanks!" said Llenn to her crack-shot partner as she rapidly backed away to avoid being caught in the demolition. If that bombardment had been twenty yards off, she could have easily gotten blown up.

"Thank you for using the Fukaziroh Grenade Service! Have a nice day!"

"Hyaaa!"

Tanya was startled by the explosion, but she was more startled by the falling debris and collapse of the building. If she hadn't made full use of her agility to withdraw, she'd have been flattened by a piece of rubble about the size of a human being.

The building collapsed with a spectacular crash. The world was dyed a deeper gray shade than before as another dust cloud enveloped Tanya where she retreated, about a hundred feet away behind the street.

Thankfully, *GGO* was a virtual world. In a real environment, she'd be in agony, choking on airborne particles. But vision still worked the same way—and Tanya couldn't see a thing.

But it's the same for Llenn, too!

She decided not to make any mistakes by moving. Instead, she lowered herself down. Even in this situation, a bullet line shone as clear as a laser, so she watched carefully for one coming through the dust and was just as careful not to touch the Bizon's trigger to make one of her own.

After twenty seconds of clattering and crumbling, the sound of the building collapsing finally faded. There couldn't be anything left to fall apart. There were a few last individual sounds of objects dropping, and then all was silent.

Then it was broken again by the return of the wind, now that the building's collapse increased the ventilation of the area. It helped the dust cloud clear faster.

Once the floating debris was gone, it would be time to fight Llenn.

Tanya prepared herself to charge for a close-range battle. There was no building between them now. Llenn couldn't call in any more grenades, surely. It would blow her up, too.

But at that point, a doubt crept in amid Tanya's determination. *What if Llenn ran away?*

What would she do if Llenn used the dust as an opportunity to scamper off to safety?

If the cloud cleared and the only thing left was Tanya herself, baring her fangs in anticipation of combat, she'd look pretty stupid. It wouldn't be odd for Llenn to do that; she often fought in utterly unorthodox ways.

The dust thinned out to the point that the side of the far building became visible. In another five seconds, everything would be clear again.

Prrrrrraaaaaaaaaaa!

There was a rattle of high-pitched, high-speed gunfire, and Tanya instantly dropped to the ground.

It was the sound of a P90 firing, a sound she heard from very close by in SJ1. She would never mistake it.

Ah-ha-ha-ha! Tanya smirked to herself upon learning that Llenn hadn't run away.

Then she realized Llenn was shooting in a different direction— not at Tanya at all. However she made this mistake, Llenn was shooting completely the wrong way.

Tanya started to run through the clearing dust. Her destination was the P90 that was the source of the rattling. She didn't need to see it to know. Her target was in the direction of the sound.

At full auto, the P90 fell silent in exactly 3.4 seconds.

But she already knew where it was. It was directly in front of her, about sixty feet away.

Tanya lifted the Bizon, and at the moment that her finger touched the trigger, a final gust of wind completely swept the cloud away.

"Ah…"

She saw the P90, pinched in between pieces of rubble.

It was fixed in place with another piece of rubble placed on top, over Llenn's hat—and a string pulled on the trigger.

Uh-oh. Oh no, this is bad, Tanya thought.

And then she heard the sound of a knife whistling through empty air behind her.

Got her!

Llenn charged, her short hair waving in the open as she swiped sideways at the back of Tanya's neck.

She should have been able to finish her off in one clean hit.

"Kyah!"

But the damage mark only appeared on the side of Tanya's head as she squealed in an oddly adorable way.

Risa Kusunoki's natural reflexes, the sharpness of her senses in hearing the sound of the approaching object, and Tanya's high agility stat together saved her life. It was a light cut to her head that cost her about 10 percent of her hit points.

I didn't finish her! That's bad!

Llenn didn't have a next move in mind.

Her plan had been to set up the P90 without the silencer and to pull the trigger with a string to make it fire at random. Once Tanya approached, drawn by the sound, she would sneak up from behind with the knife and end her.

The scheme had worked beautifully, except for Tanya dodging at the last possible moment.

Even though Llenn went to the trouble of taking off her cute pink boots so she could sneak more quietly. Her socks were pink, too.

But while Tanya exhibited tremendous reflexes in the heat of the moment, so did Llenn.

She went for a body blow against Tanya when the other girl ducked. If Tanya fired at her, Llenn would be helpless with just her knife.

Despite her tiny size, the moment was enough to knock over Tanya, whose reflexes were a bit dulled from the pain of her head. Once the other girl was knocked onto her back, Llenn straddled her stomach.

She plunged the knife downward, right for the enemy's silver eyes, trying to stab her right there.

"Shaaa!"

Swish!

Without hesitation or mercy, Llenn added her right hand to the left to increase the force of the downward stab.

Clank!

It met a gun.

Tanya pushed the Bizon up to defend herself. She held it sideways in both hands, using it like a metal bat in an attempt to block Llenn's knife.

Swish, clank! Swish, clank! Swish, clank!

Llenn stabbed again, trying to get the knife in *somewhere*, but Tanya blocked it with the Bizon three more times. They were so quick that the exchange took less than two seconds.

On the fourth stab of the knife, Tanya pushed up with the Bizon—not to block it but to knock the knife away.

That was the trap.

"Naaa!"

Llenn only pretended to stab, pulling her arms and knife inward partway down. That left Tanya's Bizon nowhere to go but farther upward.

"Taaa!"

And Llenn used her left hand to punch it from below in an uppercut.

"Ouch!"

Her fist glowed with damage, losing about 5 percent of her health. In the real world, she would have broken some fingers for sure.

But Tanya did not let go of the Bizon, preventing her beloved gun from getting jarred loose. It left her arms fully extended, however, and that gave Llenn room to slip her whole body through, like a cat.

They were in full contact. It might as well be a lover's embrace.

"Gotcha!" Llenn swung the knife in her right hand at the left side of Tanya's neck.

"Fnya!" Tanya shrieked and used her final gasp to stop the attack.

"Glergh!"

She used all her strength to pull the Bizon back toward her body—meaning against Llenn's back. Tiny little Llenn was trapped between Tanya's arms and the firm rod of metal connecting them.

"Hrrg!" Her knife fell short, just an inch away from bare skin. "Aaargh! Let goooo!"

Llenn raged and struggled, but her upper half was completely trapped on Tanya's chest, including her arms.

"Why would I do that?!" Tanya squeezed without mercy. She had the height and the strength to outclass Llenn.

"Urrrggghhh!" The smaller woman writhed but could not break free from her prison.

They were completely locked in an immobile embrace among the ruined buildings.

"Wha—?! Hey! I can't! Mo—! Erk! Muhagk!" Llenn gasped, losing her grip on language.

"You're...not...going...anywhere!" Tanya smirked ferociously.

The only thing Llenn could move was her neck, which she lifted as far back as she could, until Tanya's face was right in front of hers. Their lips were close. They did not kiss.

"Hrrg! Hey, I don't have time to roll around here hugging you!" Llenn complained.

"If I let go, my life will be in danger, so we'll just have to stay like this! Until death do us part!"

"No thanks!"

Flop. Flop, flop, flop.

Llenn tried kicking her legs, but Tanya was a full five or six inches taller, so it was pointless. All she did was stir up a bunch of empty virtual air.

"Ugh…"

There was nothing Llenn could do now. She was trapped.

Nothing, that is, except call for help.

"I'm captured here! Help me!"

Through the comm, she heard Pitohui's calm and collected voice reply, "Gosh, we're pretty swamped over here, too. Can't you do something on your own?"

A few dozen seconds earlier, shortly after Fukaziroh's initial grenade launch, Pitohui and M were on the move.

They ran down a major street through the ruined city. Their destination was SHINC's ambush point.

M had a shield panel in each hand, blocking attacks from directly ahead. Obviously, that meant he couldn't hold a gun.

Pitohui had M's M14 EBR steadied against her shoulder as she followed him. What about her KTR-09? It was stuck into the open zipper of the backpack holding the rest of M's shield. That way, she could pull it out and fire it if needed.

"I was hoping we'd have a car, but oh well. Run, M, run!"

"Grrr…"

M was slower than Pitohui, so he was pumping his legs as fast as he could.

Fukaziroh's second attack exploded on SHINC's hiding spot, but that certainly couldn't have blown them all up. If anything, it was better that it didn't.

Pitohui told Fukaziroh, "All right, don't shoot for a while. Give us a chance to shine."

"Enjoy yourselves!"

M was running up on an intersection. If they turned right, SHINC would be ahead of them in about a thousand feet.

"There we go! Keep forging ahead! Do not fear death!" she declared with the most brilliant of smiles.

"Grrr!" M would do anything Pitohui told him to do. He plunged toward the intersection where a shooter might be waiting for him at any time.

And then he got shot at like hell.

While watching out for their rear, SHINC emerged from the building they were hiding in, spotted M coming through the intersection, and unleashed a curtain of hellfire from machine guns and sniper rifles.

Rosa fired her PKM in short bursts, and in between them, Anna's and Tohma's Dragunovs delivered carefully aimed sniper shots. If M had been a split second late to hunch down, he'd have been blasted to pieces.

Ka-ka-ka-ka-kang! His thick arms held up against the hail of bullets drumming on his shields.

"Haaah!"

As soon as the machine guns paused and the bullet lines were gone, Pitohui jumped up and fired the M14 EBR over his shoulder. She had to duck back down again just as quickly, so she didn't actually see what happened.

"I think I hit 'em!"

"Gah!"

A bullet passed through Anna's left hand, and the Dragunov fell to the ground.

Rosa raised the firing frequency of the PKM to keep Pitohui from peeking out from the shield again. The machine gun's curtain of lead surrounded the two shields.

Tohma kept her scope locked on the target, determined to pick off Pitohui the next time she tried to pop up. She shouted, "The two of us will hold them down! Everyone else, flank them!"

"We can't! It's too far!" said Boss, who was flat on the street, firing her Vintorez. Holding down an enemy with covering fire so you could get to their sides or rear was a cornerstone of infantry combat, but in this case, it would mean running an entire city block. That would take too long to work. If the two of them were able to ride it out and break free, the whole idea was ruined.

"C'mon, Sophie! I'll shoot!" Boss commanded. Despite the imminent danger, Sophie stood up and rushed to Boss's position. Boss clutched the gigantic PTRD-41 her teammate was carrying.

She didn't have the sniping aim of Tohma or Anna, but she was still sharp enough to use the Vintorez. She hunched onto the ground, placing the scope over the sight line to the distant target, and zeroed in on the shield standing in the road.

Through the lens, she saw the bullet circle contract, and just as she was about to place it over the shield—Pitohui leaped out from behind it.

"Hngf!"

"You're aiming too hard!"

Pitohui bounced high and far to the right of M's shield position.

She didn't get shot. SHINC's gunners were aiming too closely at the shield itself. Pitohui knew that because of their bullet lines, of course.

Before the other team could react, Pitohui fired the M14 EBR standing up, right at Boss.

"Rrgh!"

It was Sophie who got shot through the stomach.

She leaped sideways in front of the bullet line pointing at Boss, and got shot. In fact, she dived specifically *to get* hit.

While Sophie was still in the air, Boss's aim at the shield was complete, and she pulled the trigger at the moment the circle was at its smallest.

There was a phenomenal blast of sound, and the antitank rifle's projectile took off at a height of one foot off the ground.

It struck M's shield.

As Pitohui leaped into a nearby building whose exterior glass windows were broken, out of the corner of her eye, she caught sight of the left of M's two shield panels getting blown away. There was a metallic scream loud enough to hurt the ears, and the fairly heavy panel simply flew off out of her range of vision to the left as easily as a piece of paper in the wind.

At the same time, M's thick left arm was bent at an impossible angle, and red damage light shone from his shoulder. In real life, his arm would be broken, dislocated, or both.

What's more, if it weren't massive, muscular M, that arm could easily have been ripped off and cast away with the shield, wherever it landed. His body itself got pushed backward, and he managed to fall to the right, keeping his hold on the remaining protective piece.

"Rrgh…"

With the other shield in front of him, M twisted his body so he could face SHINC's direction. Barely in time, he held up the barrier diagonally to block the shots coming for him.

Upon seeing M defending himself from a withering hail of PKM and Dragunov bullets with nothing but one arm and the backpack, Pitohui exclaimed, "Uh-oh, that's not good!"

She reached into the pouch she kept around her back. "At this rate, they're going to shoot my gun!"

Then she grabbed a cylinder and threw it as hard as she could with just the motion of her arm. The spray-can-like smoke grenade flew through the air and began to belch out its contents.

Within moments, the street was full of smoke as black as Pitohui's soul.

A thick cloud blocked the view.

"Smoke, huh…?"

Boss finished reloading the PTRD-41.

If you fired it while it was secured on the bipod, the gun's characteristic auto-discharge function powered by its own recoil would not work properly. Moving the large, heavy bolt to load the next bullet had to be done manually.

But she couldn't do it as well as Tohma, and by the time she had the scope on M's shield again, there was black smoke blocking her vision. She decided not to waste the bullet, and checked on her teammates' HP instead.

Anna was at 80 percent, still green. Only her hand was harmed, making it a light wound.

Sophie was at 10 percent. She was in grave condition, firmly in the red zone. But if anything, it might be considered lucky that she was still alive after being shot through the core with a 7.62 mm bullet. Her gauge was already blinking, meaning she'd used her med kit and was in the slow process of healing.

And Tanya was at 90 percent. She'd been speaking through the comm now and then, but out of context, her statements were very hard to parse. What was happening with her?

With the smoke for cover, M crawled forward with one arm toward Pitohui's building to the side. He'd lost one shield, taken damage on his left arm, and suffered a few shots to his elbow and feet when they became exposed. His health was at about 60 percent now.

"Hi, darling. Good job out there. Can you stand up?" Pitohui said kindly. But when she reached out and pulled him upright, she grabbed the injured left arm instead.

"Gaaah!"

"Oops, sorry."

"Hrrg…"

As soon as he was on his feet, M used a med kit on himself.

Pitohui checked her watch. 1:38.

At that very moment, Llenn called out, "I'm captured here! Help me!"

Now really wasn't the time, so Pitohui replied, "Gosh, we're pretty swamped over here, too. Can't you do something on your own?"

That's so messed up! Llenn thought. Pitohui didn't consider her plea for help in the least.

"Boss, I've got Llenn! Near the dead end to the north! Can you make it?" Tanya said right near her ear.

Tanya's next statement was "Okay. Got it," so Llenn's initial assumption was that they wouldn't be coming right away. There was still a chance.

She decided to hit up Fukaziroh for help again.

"Fuka! Tanya's caught me! Help!"

"Huhhh? What happened?" exclaimed Fukaziroh, who couldn't see the situation, of course.

Llenn had no choice but to explain, even though Tanya could hear her. "We were grappling, and she caught me in a lock. I can't get myself loose!"

"Ahhh, how very passionate. Look, there's nothing wrong with girls having a little fun."

"Yes, there is! If anyone else from SHINC comes along, I'm an easy target. I don't want to embarrass myself by dying like this!"

"Ah, I see. Where's your location?"

"Very close to the last spot! About a hundred feet north!"

"Got it. Any other last words?"

"Yeah—don't shoot me!"

"Darn."

And so Llenn just barely avoided the ignoble death from above by grenade.

Oof, there's nothin' I can do...

Fukaziroh stared at the rising smoke in the distance.

She couldn't provide backup bombardment for Llenn.

Pitohui turned down her bombardment offer; that order hadn't been rescinded yet.

Fukaziroh was left all alone on the rooftop with nothing to do.
This is so boring. I'm so bored. Can I fix some tea or something?
She shook her head and looked at the scene around her.
"Hmm?"

There was a Humvee. It was on the southern edge of the city, at
the corner of the street. About 450 yards away. It wasn't moving.

She'd looked around for the sake of security when she came up
here, and there was no car like that at the time. She would have
reported it to Pitohui, so she was certain it was new.

That left two possibilities.

Number one: As time progressed, it popped into existence as a
usable item.

Number two: An enemy had driven it here. It was far enough
away that she couldn't tell with the naked eye if anyone was
inside it.

Either way, I guess I'll blow it up. I'm bored.

It was barely at the edge of her range of accuracy, but she had
the extra advantage of being atop the building. The occasional
gusts of wind would be bothersome, but they were calm for the
moment. Even if she missed, she could just use all six of the pack.
They would come back, anyway.

To ease her boredom, Fukaziroh lifted Leftania, which was full
of normal grenades. She rested the edge of the launcher on the
rooftop handrail and placed her finger on the trigger.

When the bullet circle appeared, she moved it over to the distant Humvee, got it right on top—and then it shifted away.

Hmm? Was that the wind? she wondered.

At that very moment, a bullet hit her chest and penetrated
through to the back.

"Gahk!"

Llenn heard Fukaziroh scream. In the corner of her vision, the
hit point bar for her teammate was dropping fast.

"Fuka? What happened? Fuka?" she called, momentarily for-
getting her own predicament.

"I've been...shot... Hyaaa!"

"Fuka?"

"Llenn, this is ba—"

Boom!

A tremendous explosion drowned out Fukaziroh's voice. Her hit points dropped further.

That wasn't an insta-kill, was it? Llenn thought with terror. But the decrease did stop, leaving Fukaziroh with less than 20 percent. She was in the red zone.

It wasn't clear exactly what had happened, but it *was* clear what Llenn should do now.

"Tanya!"

"Whuh?"

The other woman faltered under the sudden glare.

"Enemies! We gotta run away!"

"Huh? Huh?"

"Just let go of me! I won't slice you! We're all going to get killed by another team coming to scoop us up! Hurry!"

"......"

Faltering from Llenn's intensity, Tanya's grip loosened, and Llenn wriggled out of her Bizon trap like a desperate cat. She had the opportunity to slash at Tanya's neck, but she did not. She returned the knife to her waist.

With a quick movement of her left hand, Llenn returned her boots to her feet from inventory. Then she ran back to the P90 and hat and picked them up.

"Run away, Pito! I think another enemy's coming up from the south!" she said as she plopped her cap back on her head. There was no response.

Instead, as if to answer the obvious question, she saw Pitohui's and M's hit points dropping at a precipitous rate.

"Boss! Llenn says enemies are coming!" Tanya said to her teammate.

Boss's answer was "Yeah...I know..."

Boss watched it happen.

As the smoke cleared, in the distance down the long, straight road, a Humvee approached at blazing speed and came to a rapid stop just fifty yards or so from the building where Pitohui and M were sheltering.

And from the bulletproof roof turret of the vehicle, they began to fire.

Vraaaaaaaaa!

A bright flash emitted from the edge of the turret, accompanied by a sound like a deep, snarling buzzer.

The flashing was, of course, the muzzle of the gun firing, but it did not let up. It did not flicker. It was constantly alight.

Continuous sound and continuous muzzle flashing. An endless stream of orange tracer lights led to the first floor of the building.

"That's an M134 Minigun...," Boss murmured.

Even in the gun-packed world of *GGO*, there was nothing else that could shoot with that kind of mad abandon.

The M134 was a Gatling gun, a ring of identical barrels that spun at high speed on a motorized system, loading and firing all the while.

With the aid of the motor, the firing speed of the Minigun could reach up to four thousand rounds per minute. That was sixty-six rounds per second. If you didn't know much about ranged weapons, you might assume that was wrong by an entire digit. It was an unfathomable amount of firepower.

The M134 was called the "Minigun" because it was a scaled-down 7.62 mm version of an aircraft armament called the M61A1 Vulcan, but the barrels and motor alone made it nearly forty pounds, so it was one of the heaviest weapons in *GGO*.

In practical terms, it was basically impossible to use while held in the real world, but you saw big macho guys shooting them from the waist in action movies. That was possible in *GGO*, too. The game's developers probably knew that people would *want* to do it after seeing it in movies. Therefore, it was a weapon only for extreme enthusiasts, because it required maximum strength just to be able to use in that clumsy way.

It was so heavy that it was hard to walk while carrying—but set up in the turret of an armored Humvee was a different story altogether.

With the mobility of tires, the protection of armored body and glass, and the firepower to shoot dozens of times a second, this was a strength the average character couldn't possibly hope to counteract.

But Boss didn't think that was unfair.

If you could bring the weapon into the game, you could use it. And one of the core concepts of finding vehicles in *GGO* and Squad Jam was "finders keepers, losers weepers."

But seeing Pitohui and M under a hail of fire in the building, and probably being turned into mincemeat, Boss felt a bit more conflicted now.

It was obvious the other guys were from the allied team—one of those masked groups lounging around atop the ice, with their weapons tucked away in their virtual inventory. They must have seen that SHINC was struggling with LPFM and come to help. It might be the proper choice when considering team play.

But Boss spat, "Dammit... Mind your own business."

She didn't want anyone's help, even if her own team was going to die. It was no longer a fair and proper fight. How could she possibly apologize to Llenn's side?

The roaring of the Minigun came to a stop.

The actual firing was only for three seconds at most, but that meant nearly two hundred 7.62 mm rounds fired into the building. Dust billowed out from the interior. Pitohui and M were almost surely dead by now.

"I'm going to go have a word with them!" Boss said, getting to her feet.

Just then, she heard Tanya cry, "Boss! Llenn says enemies are coming!"

Then the Humvee's turret slowly rotated so that the Minigun was facing *them*. Bullet lines extended toward her own chest.

"Yeah...I know..."

The muzzle of the Minigun flashed.

To be continued...

AFTERWORD
Gun Gale Diary: Part 8

Hello, everyone. I'm the author of this book, Keiichi Sigsawa.

It's been two months since the release of Volume 7. Has anything changed in your life?

Sword Art Online Alternative Gun Gale Online (hereafter, "the series") has reached its eighth volume! I'm so happy.

And that means this "Afterword *Gun Gale* Diary," where the author can write whatever he feels like, has also reached its eighth installment.

For the afterwords of the previous seven volumes, I discussed how this series came about, my favorite guns, the length of my second toes (which I spoke about quite a bit), my recipe for pork sukiyaki, the tools one needs to change a tire, a very simple three-minute method for creating world peace, and that this series is becoming an anime. It's been a wide-ranging segment beloved by all. And this time, the topic of choice is "the very first middle volume of my life."

Why am I talking about middle volumes? I think you've all figured it out by now, haven't you?

Yes, it's because putting this book out in August meant I didn't have enough time to write it all into a two-part story! Mostly because I was so incredibly busy with anime stuff.

In the afterword of the previous volume, I wrote, "What will happen in the second half?" as though this would definitely be the conclusion of Squad Jam. Well, it turns out that was a lie. Sorry.

While we're at it, the first installment of the "Afterword *Gun Gale* Diary" was actually in the previous volume. I'm glad no one realized this. *(Editor's note: You're the only one who thinks that.)*

Anyway, that was a very long intro to saying, this is the middle volume. The fourth Squad Jam will continue for one more book.

I've done two-part story arcs many times before in my career, but this will be my first three-parter. It's been a brand-new experience for me. It's very novel.

Why is it so novel, you might ask?

It's because by the time the reactions from the first volume come in, the last volume is still being written, so I can take those opinions into account and make alterations to the content if I want.

In my case, whenever I had a two-book story, by the release date of the first novel, I had pretty much written the entire second one already. Naturally, it would be impossible to make any major changes at that point—even if there were a few minor things in the proofreading stages.

Now, when people started issuing their reactions to the first volume...

Oops, hang on. Let me be clear here: If you haven't read the first part yet, please do not read any further. It would be a major spoiler.

Of course, there will be no spoilers about this middle volume.

Shall I proceed?

On to the reactions to the first volume...

Many, many people guessed, "I bet that at the end, Fire will be revealed to be a good guy, deep down!"

But Sigsawa is the exact kind of twisted person who wants to mess with your expectations.

So I've decided that in the final part of this story, I'll reveal that Fire was actually a "good girl" all along. Not to toot my own horn, but it's a Sigsawa staple to have characters you thought were male turn out to be female. You know, like *that* one. And the other one. You know who I'm talking about.

"I'm sure that the team of Shirley and Clarence are going to do big things," some people hoped. So I'm going to say they were actually a figment of Llenn's exhausted mind and get rid of them by the third page of the next volume. They were *never really there*. Isn't that neat?

"What if it was Pitohui who told Fire that Llenn plays *GGO* all the time?"

"What if it was Miyu?"

"What if it was the gymnastics team?"

There were lots of guesses about that one. So I'm going to say it was Llenn's niece who did it—the daughter of Karen's older sister, who lives in the same building as her. That's right, the four-year-old was the mastermind all along! No one's going to see that one coming. Not even me.

She gave Karen a clay brooch as a present. But hidden inside was a high-tech spying bug…

That's the horrifying truth contained within the third and final volume. *GGO* is about to change classes into a horror series.

Of course, I've already submitted the basic plot outline to the editorial department for the third volume—but there's still plenty of time to rewrite it so that it contains all of the above ideas. I mean, it's not at all rare for the finished story to be different from the plot outline.

In other words, whatever you think and hope will happen in

the third volume won't happen. You'll be totally blindsided. Look forward to that...and steel yourself.

If the final product doesn't turn out this way, know that there was a terrible battle between Sigsawa and the editorial department, and that your beloved author lost.

And if your hopes turned out to be correct, don't get uppity and think, "Sigsawa ripped off our ideas! Give us a little bit of that royalty money! Or a lot of it! Here's my bank account number! You have to pay the transaction fees, too!"

I need all the money from my royalties so that I can pay all my necessary bills for taxes and rent and power, and other essential everyday items like food, clothes, and model air guns.

But if any of you *do* correctly guess what will happen exactly, I'll be amazed.

I'll write up my own special certificate and award it to you for being a truly understanding and insightful reader of mine. What's that? You don't want such a thing?

Anyway, if you set up your expectations for the final part based on this volume, just assume that I've already finished writing it by now.

I started writing this *Gun Gale Online* series with Reki Kawahara's permission, and now I've reached Volume 8. I feel very fortunate and emotional about this.

Your high praise and the honor of having a TV anime has left me overjoyed.

The next book to finish this Squad Jam will be Volume 9, but if there is to be more after that, putting us into double digits, I do not yet know at this point.

But while I don't know what my plan will be, I can assure you that I will write the next volume to the utmost of my ability, and I hope you look forward to it.

That's all for this time. Let's meet again in the concluding volume of SJ4!

By the way, I intend to fill this segment by writing passionately about "how to prevent painful stubbing accidents on the corner of your shelf by starting the fashionable trend of always being in a handstand" next time. Look forward to that.

Keiichi Sigsawa

Since Karen gave up on the idea of being "cute" at a fairly young age, her concept of cuteness has aged along with her. I think this is the image she had in mind while putting together her pink outfit.

アーリー
レンちゃん
Early
Llenn

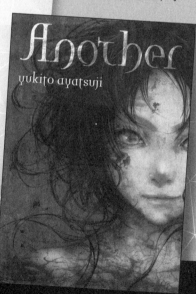